D1528274

This book formatting template was made by Cover Me design INC.

BBW LOVIN

This book is a work of fiction. Names, characters, businesses, organiza- tions, places, events and incidents either are the product of the author's imagination or are used fictitiously. Any

1

For information contact :

(PO BOX 23504 Chicago IL 60623,)

Darkberrypublications.com

Book and Cover design by Cover me Designs

ISBN:

Darkberrpublications@facebook.com

Twitter : @urbannovelist

First Edition: September 2015

3

Table of Contents

4

Acknowledgments from the heart of the

author

I WOULD LIKE TO DEDICATE THIS BOOK TO THE UNCONDITIONAL LOVE THAT IS A GIVEN FROM OUR FATHER IN HEAVEN, FOR HIS UNWAVERING UNDERSTANDING IN CONTINUING TO GIVE EACH AND EVERY ONE OF US OUR GREATNESS IN HIS IMAGE AND LIKENESS,

THE CHARACTERS WITHIN THESE PAGES DEPICT THE DAY TO DAY STRUGGLES THAT SOME IN SOCIETY HAVE HEAPED UPON US BELIEVING THAT WE MUST FIT IN TO A BOX IN ORDER TO BE ACCEPTED, INSTEAD OF LOVING SELF...

I PRAY THAT THIS STORY OPENS EYES TO EVERYONE AND EVERY READER NO MATTER WHAT AGE, RACE, AND BELIEF AND OR BODY TYPE,

THAT WITH GOD ALL THANGS ARE POSSIBLE...

FROM THE WORLD OF DARKBERRY, WE GIVE YOU OUR REALITY ON OUR CANVAS.

Author Rahim A'Sun

9

Prologue

Sitting on the edge of my desk with my hair all over my head, messy, panting, and sweating clothes ripped, I tried to get a hold of my emotions and composer but I had one of the best feelings in the world. The way this man just pleasured me was nothing less of remarkable.

How he had my plus sized body turned up into a pretzel shaped position, I will never know or will I even try to understand. He held me in different positions, that only a size 10 could muster, but I loved it.

Feeling woozy and out of breath I reached for my panties and stockings from the floor,

"Damn! Baby I love those thick hips and sexy thighs, when can I see you again?" He said as he wiped his lips of my nectar.

I wondered what it was about me he couldn't get enough of. I wasn't a model type chic with the fake ass and small waist, but all woman. With curves and dimples and a few rolls here and there and a size twenty –two in this industry was considered obese.

I didn't want to get my heart broken by one of the sexiest, wealthiest compassionate men I have met in this business. With his success and looks alone he could have his pick of any woman he wanted.

I stood up trying to hide some of my protruding belly.

"No need to hide all that sexy, let me look at you." He said holding my hands out on each side to get a full view of all of my curves and rolls as I like to call them. He smiled as if he'd seen a goddess.

I tried to place my hands over myself to cover my body, but he wasn't allowing that, in fact he kissed every inch of my breast, navel and even my chunky thighs. He lifted his eyes to see the expression on my face. Much to his shock I had tears rolling down my cheeks.

"Baby girl … whats wrong? Did I hurt you?" he asked as I snatched away to put my panties and stockings on. Once I was dressed and my clothes were tucked in neatly, I didn't say a word I turned and walked out of the door. Leaving him looking bewildered and confused.

There was no way I was going to get played, I know my role and played my part.

Chapter 1

Respecting my Curves

Girl, so tell me have you heard from Jon 'Te? Damn that man is fine as hell!"

"Yes Valerie," I said rolling my eyes upward.

"Yes I have but I'm not trying to go there, I am not going to let this man or any other man hurt me, besides I'm building my career, and who has the time for a relationship."

Valerie just shook her head at me. Judging from the curl of her lip on the left side, I knew she was getting tired of my excuses. To be honest so was I.

A part of me felt I was just as beautiful on the outside as some of the super models I manage.

My job was to sell an image, a fantasy of sex, love and romance, and in today's industry plus sized women were not the idea appearance for this.

I have never in my life been a small female, in fact, the largest I had gotten was up to a size 24. My body was not flat abs and a big butt. The biggest thing on me was my size 44dd breast, my pussy hood, and smile.

My girl Valerie and I would always joke about having a large stomach whenever one of our size 0 clients with flat abs would come into the office.

I learned a long time ago that everybody is not meant to be stick figure pretty, some of us have curves and depth to our bodies that are just as appealing to a man. In fact this pussy hood mine as

1

I refer to as my gut, has seen its share of some good dick every now and then, but every time I fall the guy always has to come way left field, he would say he hasn't had the time for a relationship or hits me with the 'it's not you, it's me 'speech, I have heard that so much until I thought I would already know the words before he speaks it out. This time, I was going to beat him to the punch.

Jon 'te Cullbirth is not the average man you would meet in a bar, in fact I met him on a dating site called 'Thick lovin smooth touchin' one of the fastest up and coming dating sites for big beautiful women such as myself. This site was made for those of us who don't have the time to meet and date on a regular because of the busy lives we lead, so this was the new and better way to either find love or some good lovin' either or it will serve a purpose.

2

We talked for a little while then we decided to meet up. The first time I saw him, I went with every intent to just say hello and a few laughs then keep it moving. This man's appearance was so fine, I could hardly stand. His light mixed with mocha and caramel skin was almost flawless. The Armani suit that defined his arms and Gucci loafers that adorned his feet had him in every sense of the word, lookin' like money. The moment he walked over to me and introduced himself in person, I knew he would be getting up in my panties that night, plus it had been a while at that time. It was something about the way he spoke, the clothes he wore and the smell of some the most expensive cologne money could buy filled our space, the personal space we had which was getting smaller by the second.

A smart, business savvy woman knows what she wants at first sight. And I wanted him. He looked at me as if his eyes were piercing through my soul. He stared for a while then asked me to have a seat, he pulled my chair from under the table and stood and I placed my round bottom in it. The compliments came back to back the whole date. It was too good to be true. In my mind if I only had a night with him, I would scratch my itch and I'd be on my way. That was four dates ago and in this short time he has been on me like white on rice, wining and dining and some great sex anywhere we can get it.

The limo, the set of a modeling photo shoot, anywhere even in the conference room.

When I think back to the times I share with him they are nothing short of amazing.

4

"Can you put those boxes up against the wall? And I will get back to you about moving the rest of them." I gave orders to the movers as I sat at my desk thinking long and hard about this man that I wish I could forget.

The fact that we are in somewhat of the same industry, on the first date after our long and satisfying session, I found out he was a sports agent to a few of New York's most talented and gifted athletes. Blake Griffin, LeBron James, Stephan Curry, and Kevin Durant are just a few he represented.

The sound of my cell phone ringing caused me to come back to my reality. I picked up my Galaxy note 4, an unfamiliar number was on a screen so I answered,

5

"Tori Graceson how may I help you?"

"Hello Ms. Graceson could you hold, I have a call from Mr. Cullbirth on line one for you." Before I could answer she placed the call on hold.

"Hello, Tori my love, how are you?" His deep sultry yet professional voice sent shivers down my spine and tingled the area down in my panties, that he knew how to stroke so well. I smiled and tried my best to stay strong, "I'm okay, just busy."

"Oh, so I see you gonna hit me with the busy speech again, look I am really feeling you everything about you Tori. Why are you playing me to the left?"

I took a deep breath and envisioned for a second his light brown eyes and full soft lips. His whole character I was feeling him as well, but in this business I have seen it too many times before, the big girls always finish last.

"JC it's not like that, I thought you were busy doing, I mean handling your business with the super model chic that you were out on a date with the other night. They had your picture plastered all over the newspaper in the whole –who section. Yes, it read, you and the lovely Ms. Eureka Georgeon have been an item for a while huh?" The jealousy I felt once I laid eyes on that article came through my tone.

"Tori, it's not what you think. Eureka and I are not in a relationship. We have to make a few appearances in public to make the company think we're a hot couple."

7

"Ooh, so that makes it okay? I sit back and look at this man, a man that I know for a fact couldn't be in love with a person like her. For starters she doesn't have, well she is pretty and nice and fit, but she can command you the way my body does. Look JC, you and I both know how this works, if the industry calls you will come running. So I will save me and you both some time. You go your way and …." I took a deep breath, "and I will go mine." I quickly hung up and got up from my desk. I couldn't take it, I was so confused, and feelings of jealousy and regret filled me to the pit of my stomach. Was I doing the right thing? Why had I just assumed this man wouldn't love me? Why, why, why.'

Thoughts consumed me so badly I bolted out of the door down to the elevator; I had to get to my car, make it home and just relax.

I got in my BMW and started the engine, for a quick second I could have sworn I'd seen someone on the other side of the garage, but when I adjusted my rear-view mirror I didn't see anyone. I placed my seat belt on and put the car in drive, as I drove toward the front to exit, suddenly a tall gentleman appeared almost out of now where with 2 huge bouquets of roses, he stood almost directly in front of my car, luckily I wasn't speeding.

"Oh my God what is wrong with you? I almost-" he held out the two large bouquets and began to sing a song, "Girl you are to me all that a woman should be, and I dedicate my life to always. Oh, girl, I want you so, I can't find enough ways to let you know, but you can be sure you'll know, I want you always."

9

Once he was done he placed the roses in my hand along with a card, I opened it up.

Tori, I know it has only been a short time, but you have touched me. You embody everything I desire and more. Will you do me the honor of coming to Mami with me for this sports conference? Before you say no, I want to proposition you, bring along your team, so that you all can pick up a few new clients while we are there. No funny business I just want to be with you Tori.

JC.

I placed the note back inside of the flowers gave the delivery person a nod then drove off. Smiling all the way I couldn't help but consider his offer. Not only will that mean some more good sexual sessions with him, but expanding my business in the process. I turned on my radio, 'I don't need you, I don't need you. But I want you. I don't mean,

10

I don't mean to, but I love you.' Jhene Aiko's hot single hit the right chords. The lyrics described how I was feeling so I turned it all the way up and sang along to all the lyrics with my mind in deep thought on what I will do next.

Chapter 2

Just my Type

"Mmm yes, stroke that dick. Mm-put that fat pussy on me girl. Yes, yes, yes. OH MY Gawd YES!"

I jumped from my bed in a cold sweat. I tried to gather my breath. I could keep Tori out of my mind now she was invading my dreams. I hoped like hell she says yes. Getting up out of the bed I placed my slippers on my feet and reached for my silk robe hanging on the chair.

"Mmm, where you going love?" a groggy yet sleepy Eureka said as she stirred the covers.

"Go ahead back to sleep I'm going to get me some water, I'm good." I talked over my shoulders, not wanting to look at her. I hated myself for giving in to what society says my ideal partner should look like.

Yes Eureka was sexy and hot as ever, any man would love seeing her on his arm, but she was just that arm and eye candy. She didn't hold a candle to Tori. Eureka is a very beautiful woman, her 5'4 frame along with her 36-24-36 brick house body was what every man adored and worshiped and women hated. But Eureka lacked the substance I needed and wanted and found in Tori.

The more I longed for Tori, the more it seemed Eureka was inserting herself into my life every chance she got. She came to my job with expensive

13

furs and things giving the illusion that I provided
her with those things, but that was far from the
truth. She got a lot of free stuff from different
companies she'd done a modeling job for. But as of
lately it seemed she noticed me making our
relationship into nothing but business, so tonight
she showed up at my front door wearing nothing
but a long fur coat, black red bottom Christian
Louboutin high heels and a smile. As soon as I
opened the door she immediately drop to her
knees, giving me some head, the more I tried to
resist the more she locked her warm wet, slippery
jaws around my nine- inch anaconda so tight , it felt
like a vacuum suction hose was on it. I She deep
throated until she almost gagged.

I reached down to pull her up so that my neighbors
don't see her on her knees with my pants down by
my ankles. That was about seven long hours ago, I
hated that I gave in to her, the fact was real that I

14

wanted something or someone else other than her, she might be fine catch for the next man, but not me.

I walked over to the cabinet and pulled out a glass, placing it on the table I filled it with ice and opened a bottle of Dasani water. My mind was all over the place, I wondered would Tori come to Mami with me next week. "Tori, Tori, Tori" I spoke her name aloud as I downed the glass of water. He face was all I could envision as Eureka rode me like a cowgirl. The moment I released my load on her stomach I didn't even look at her, kiss or even touch her. I wanted to kick myself for letting my dick decide for me which hole it wanted to hide in.

Looking over at the computer screen, I noticed I had a notification. I walked over and spend it

'I will accompany you to Miami JC, business okay. Please send me all of the details and our

15

accommodations. I think this will be a much-needed getaway/ business, Oh and all work and no play makes for an unhappy beacation. Lol

Sincerely Tori.

Smiling from ear to ear, I closed the e-mail. I was so happy that she agreed to come with me. This is more than enough time to get her to be with me. I am more determined to make this woman, this beautiful, big, curvaceous woman mine.

"Hey JC are you okay? I missed you." Eureka said as she snaked her arms around my waist. Her touch was soft and alluring, but I didn't want that from her. "Hey, I'm sorry, I wanted to get some water and check my emails, and just as I thought I have to fly to Miami to close a huge deal." I closed the top part of my laptop.

"Oh that's fine, I can come with if you like."

16

"No, that's okay I will be in meetings all week so there will be no time for any play."

"Umm, so when do you leave?" Eureka had one eyebrow raised and her face contoured in a frown.

"Eureka, you are starting to sound like we are a married couple, you and I both agreed what is was, please don't tell me you switching it up now." My words came out a little harsher than I intended them to.

She slowly removed her arms from around my waist as if she was dropping them in defeat.

"You are right, what was I thinking you and I are business and pleasure nothing more. I will go up and get dressed I have an early photo shoot." She quickly turned on her heels and ran up the stairs the fact I didn't stop her seemed to infuriate her.

17

Instead, I sat down at my computer and replied to Tori. My heart and mind was on one thing, until Eureka came back down the stairs with her fur coat, shoes, and a wicked smile, "look JC I know you are a busy man, and can have any woman you want , I mean look at you, those well-toned abs, broad shoulders and light, smooth and captivating skin." She snaked her way over and stood in front of me. In a swift motion, she opened her coat, the scent of jasmine and lavender pleasantly invaded my nostrils.

Naked as the day she was born she placed one foot on the table and spread her pussy lips apart, exposing her pink clit. She began dipping her fingers in and out of her pussy, each time she would bring them out, she would lick all of her nectar. "Mmm you sure you don't want to taste it, I promise it tastes good," she moaned in delight as she continued to pleasure herself.

18

My manhood rose to attention as she dove deeper and licked her fingers seductively. She moaned and released sounds of pleasure until I wanted in on the party. I got up and roughly bent her over the couch, then rammed my manhood deep inside of her, "you want this dick you nasty lil bitch? Take it, take it. Ya lil slut." I rapidly thrust my hips until my ball were covered with her juices.

"Yes, yes, daddy, fuck me, make me your nasty bitch, and fuck this pussy. Come on JC stop being a pussy boy."

I sped up until sweat and tears of pleasure were running down her face. AHH! AHHH! YES! YES! FUCK ME! She screamed and moaned until her voice was raspy. I continued my pace, with every thrust I wanted to punish her, I wanted Tori's curves and soft skin, but right now I will take it out on Eureka until I released a huge load of cum onto

her back, hair and ass.   The moment I was done
she didn't say a word, instead she wobble over to
the front door and walked out, leaving me right
there on the couch confused and out of breath.

She wasn't going to make this easy.

Chapter 3

Know Your Role and Do your Part

The office was buzzing as Tori and her staff prepared to take on a whole new list of aspiring models.

When she got the confirmation and all of the details from JC her heart skipped two beats. This man was the real deal and wasn't giving up getting her to be his.

There she sat at her desk shuffling papers and moving huge stacks of model's portfolios, she had

21

gotten a spike in new faces hungry to be America's most sought after face.

"Val, have you seen the folder for Missy Rose? I could have sworn I put it ri-"she looked over the huge pile right into the smiling face of Eureka. Tori tried to conceal her unpleasant attitude for her, instead she plastered a phony smile, "Hello, welcome to Asiatic Complexions how can I help you." Tori stood up right fixing her dress. It was as if she didn't want Eureka to see her in a less than perfect light.

"Hello, my name is Eureka George and I am looking for some new representation, but im quite sure you all know who I am." She hung her hand in a downward position as if she was telling Tori to kiss it. Tori looked her up and down, but wouldn't give her the gratification of letting her know she knew exactly who she was, so Tori shook her hand, "no I

22

haven't had the pleasure , what did you say your name was again? How many ads or movies have you been in?" Tori held a slight smirk.

"Umm, well I am the internationally known cover model for "Tories' the hottest magazine for gentlemen. Eureka replied rolling her eyes up toward the ceiling. Eureka thought to herself 'this is the fat bitch he wants? Wow a shame he needed to down grade.

Without being asked Eureka shoved some folders that were sitting on the seat to the floor and sat down.

"Oh Im sorry, I didn't mean to make a mess." She said with a sarcastic chuckle. "Anyway I need some new jobs for this next week preferably in Miami." Eureka smirked from ear to ear, judging the expression on Tori's face Eureka had just hit a nerve. Eureka crossed one leg on top of the other,

23

in a defiant manner. Tori swallowed the lump that

formed in her throat. Inwardly she counted down

too ten, she didn't want this skinny stick figure of a

female to take her out of her professional

character. She studied Eureka a brief but in depth

moment, she realized she said this to get to her.

While Eureka was at Jc's, she stood and watched

him type the email back to Tori about the Miami

trip. Just like a female detective she stood quiet and

read, when JC was getting ready to type back to her

again that's when she startled him, but by then she

had all the information she needed.

"Okay, Miami, let me see...well I don't have

anything this coming week but what I can do is get

your portfolio together first, you do have one on

hand don't you?"

"But of course, I have an older head shot, I've been

meaning to update it, but with my busy schedule

24

along the fact my man loves, I mean simply loves all of me, I haven't had the time to get anything done, you know what im talkin bout girl friend." Eureka laughed loud as if she heard a joke, Tori on the other hand tried her best to hold her composure.

"Oh perhaps you have heard of him? We were featured last month in the who's- who society page of the Tribune. Oh I have the clip right here" she placed the article on top of Tori's desk. Smiling from ear to ear as she watched Tori's reaction, "yes JC is a remarkable man, and we have been dating about a year now. I think he is the one, oh my God the way he puts it down, makes me want to destroy this perfect body just to have his baby."

Tori's professional demeanor was nearly gone, until she picked up the folder with Eureka's portfolio and head shot inside. She smiled at her and held the article in front of her. She thought since this woman *wants to play games she would show her how it's done.*

"I tell you what, Eureka I am impressed about your experience, and I tell you what I will have you accompany me and my models down to Miami this week coming. I can see you becoming a huge success. Stand up right quick again, okay remove your coat let me take a body shot of you with my IPhone 6, Girl the resolution on this camera is top of the line, I want to send this to out photography staff."

Eureka eagerly stood up and began to pose, Tori snapped picture after picture. Just like Tori thought this female was so shallow about her looks until she couldn't even see that the plan she came in with had now been turned on her.

Eureka pulled the scarf from around her neck, to give a sexier facial pose exposing a huge passion

26

mark on her neck. Tori eyes lit up Eureka noticed that Tori seen the passion mark, "oh sorry, me and JC had a little fun last night. I thought I'd put enough make-up on to cover it." Eureka smiled and cockily played with the camera, evident that Tori was rattled.

Eureka push the knife in deeper as she posed and toyed with tori she continued to talk about hers and Jc's relationship. The fact that he was just almost harassing her into coming to Miami with him and the same time was sexing her was a little too much for Tori, so she ended her makeshift photo shoot with Eureka and promised to call her with the itinerary and hotel they would all be staying in. Eureka even told Tori she would pay for her own air fare and accommodations.

27

Tori fought every urge she had to pick up that phone and call JC to cancel, but she weighed her options, on one hand her business would see more and more clientele once they got to Mami and JC would use all of his resources to plug her in, not to mention the fact groupies hang around those events just to sleep with the ballers, so that was a plus for her and her company to gain more and more jobs. She put her desk phone back down and turned the lamp off, got up and walked out of the office all up in her emotions.

Chapter 4

Why is it that good girls finish last.....

I came in my apartment consumed and a little hurt. I really didn't want this to get this far with JC. I knew in my heart a man like him could never love, I mean truly love a woman like me. I placed my keys on the table next to my briefcase. I sat down for a second and pulled out all of the files I needed to go over before this trip. I had to weed out who would be going and who I can send to a photo shoot in England in the same week. As soon as I pulled out the stack of folders, Eureka's picture hit the table as if it was right on Que. I rolled my eyes, "that skinny bitch." I said aloud as I held her picture in my hand. I slammed it down on the table and went and got a tall crystal glass from the cupboard.

Walking toward the refrigerator to get some Ice, I cursed the day I allowed myself to feel deeper than I should have for JC. I poured myself a tall glass with ice of apple juice. Then I grabbed some leftover chicken Alfredo, garlic bread, corn and a slice of homemade lemon pound cake. I sat down at the table with my comfort food.

I took a big scope of the pasta, then drank a gulp of apple juice. Just as I was about to put my fork into the lemon cake, I caught a glimpse of myself in the mirror on the wall of the fore. I took a long glance almost disgusted with myself that I'd let this stick figure bitch ruin my low carb diet.

I wanted to change the way I looked and I started with what and how much I was eating. I pushed the plate away and stood up to look directly in the
30

mirror. I could see the beauty in my face, but the sadness spoke louder.

I reminisced back to when I was younger, I had always been a heavier female. I have one of those imperfect thick bodies that some men loved and most women laughed at or felt I could never compare to them, especially if they were a size two.

But it all came to a halt when I turned sixteen there was this young man, Jermaine 'J-Dog' Horton, and I was really feeling him. We'd been dating for a while. He was my first love. He always told me he loved me and I was his everything.

There was nothing like that teenage love, the kind of love that would make you damn near wanna kill your mother. Anyway, the day my whole world came crashing down was the day I snuck one of his lettermen jackets out of his house and wore it to school.

When I stepped in the school with his letterman jacket and a pair of all white- air force ones, some form fitting white skinny jeans and a screen T with the word 'FLAWLESS' written on the front.

I walked through the halls to home room, smiling and happy. I'd just spoken with Jermaine the night before on the phone like we always did until the wee hours of the morning. He was sitting on the desk talking and laughing with a group of his friends. I never hung around them because my momma would kill me if she knew I had a boyfriend or that I have had sex. I'd always kept us a secret, there was no way I wanted my mother getting wind of me and his relationship and make me end it. I watched for a little while as he laughed and joked until I saw Janessa, the school slut. She was known to give up the cookie to any boy who gave her the time or day. To say she was an easy fuck would be an understatement. When I watched her and her girls sashay their slender, big breast having asses walked over towards him and his friends, I jumped up and rushed over to make my presence known. At first I was just going to sit there because he hadn't noticed I was even in the room.

With one of my girls close with me, I walked up and stood on the side of the desk.

"Hey Jermaine boo, how you doing," Janessa said in a seductive coo.

He was smiling from ear to ear until he noticed me standing there with a frown on my face.

"He...Hey, Nessa." He nervously said.

"Yea, Jermaine boo." I sarcastically said with my hand on my hip.

Janessa and her crew caught on to my stance of me claiming what was mine, Jermaine. They looked at each other than at me and started laughing. I looked at Jermaine who'd just lowered his eyes as these females laughed like they'd just heard a Kat Williams joke. They laughed and laughed speaking to each other in a whisper as they stared at me.

"So this what the fuck you want Jermaine?" I said as tears began to wail up in my eyes. His silence spoke loud, but I was so in love I couldn't believe he played me like that. Instead, he just turned his back as if I wasn't standing there.

"Yea, he knows what's well and what's not. Did you think this fine ass man would want yo fat ass? Fat bitch please stay in your lane." Janessa laughed in my face as Jermaine sat there. I could see in his

34

eyes he wanted to say something to defend me, but he allowed peer pressure and his friends to take me down.

"You know what Nessa? You are right his nothing ass could never have a big fine sexy bitch like me, yeah the only thing he is good for is a skinny ugly faced easy fuck type of bitch like you." She lunged at me with her fist landing right in my eye. There was a tussle and I ended up on top of her, "help, help get this big bitch off of me." She yelled.

"Stop Tori! You gonna kill her. Stop!" I heard Jermaine say as he pulled me off of her.

"Tori, baby please stop!"

"Oh, so now Really? You just sat her while her and her little friends dogged me out. You said you loved me. I guess I'm only good to love behind closed

35

doors. I love you and this is what you really think of me."

"Tori! To-" he called out as I stormed off. Tears streaming down my face. Could I hear his friends laughing saying stuff like "you been smashin'' her fat ass? Damn nig how it was fuckin a whale." They laughed and laughed and all I could do was run out of there.

Later that day he called and called my phone. Even sent me a few emails. I sat in my room crying and ripping his jacket to pieces.

After that year, I stayed my distance until I went away to college. It took me a while to recognize my self-worth. I stayed trying the new fads and diets to look like a skinny model with a perfect body and flawless skin, it was until I almost killed myself-trying a new diet.

Throughout my college years, I dated dog after dog. Each one was no better than the next. The ones who really wanted me showed it behind closed doors, but in public, I guess they allowed society to be their deciding factor.

It took years before I could learn to love me, Tori. For who and what I was.

Feelin those old self-esteem issues brewing up, I walked over to the mini bar I had in my living room.

I opened a bottle of EJ brandy, but quickly closed it, remembering the horrible headache I had after we drank that on a girl's night. I picked up a bottle of Everclear, this was the strongest alcohol I had in my house. I looked around for another glass and filled it with ice with no chaser straight up I Just swallow a big gulp of the Everclear. My chest burned as it eased its way down my throat.

37

"Damn! That shit rockin." I held back the urge to spit it all out, I wanted to escape this feeling, the same feelings that almost destroyed me years ago. Instead, I let it burn a little more then downed another glass. I took gulp after gulp until I noticed the bottle was half empty. I was starting to sway as I tried to stand up.

The room seemed like it was spinning. "Damn light weight. Can't handle your liquor." I said aloud as I reach for my glass and cell phone.

I clumsily dialed the one person's number who was invading my thoughts and mood.

"Hello ...hello. Oh, I didn't hear your ass answer, anyway I wanna tell you a few things." The spit held, was flying all over the place.

"You, you fundoshi, bastard I hope you ri-oot." I was starting to get so drunk that I couldn't see my hand in front of my face.

I reached out for the glass of everclear, "see this is why good sisters. . . Big fine as sister like me always go last. Your woman came by my office today JC, or shall I say Mr. Jon 'te Cullbirth, oh Eureka George's future baby daddy. And to think that I thought you were different." I rambled on and on until I heard a beep. This whole time I'd been rambling to his voicemail.

I threw my cell phone on the floor. I walked over to my cd player and turned it on,

"Mama said, you're a pretty girl what's in your head it doesn't matter

Brush your hair, fix your teeth, what you wear is all that matters. Just another stage, Pageant the pain

39

away, this time I'm gonna take the crown, without falling down, down. Pretty hurts, shine the light on whatever's worse, perfection is the disease of a nation, Pretty hurts, Shine the light on whatever's worse tryna fix something

But you can't fix what you can't see, It's the soul that needs the surgery."

The lyrics to one of Beyoncé's soul-stirring songs, 'Pretty Hurts', hit me right to the core.

For years, I have struggled with my inner demons, about my weight or lack of this pretty, that society deems it to be. To me, I was Tori and that should be enough. Not the fake breast or bottoms to match and the IQ even lower than the breast cup, but pretty enough to be accepted.

"Pre...tt...y hurts... pre...e...e...tt...y...y hurts, you ain't Neva lied B." I tried singing loud and off-key as

I downed the last of my drink then slid to the floor, as my tears stained my shirt and anger soiled my soul.

The next morning, the sun peeked through my window burning my eyes as I opened them to wake up, everything was a blur. I moved my leg thinking I was about to get out of bed, but my arm was stiff and there were no bed or covers, I was half naked on the floor. I tried to part my lips, dry and cracking, and the taste was like I'd eaten some cat shit or something. I reached out and got a firm grip on the wall.

41

Slowly I stood up trying to gain my balance. I remembered bits and pieces but not the full night. I looked over at the table where my half eaten meal still sat. I started feeling nauseated and rushed over to the nearest sink, I felt my last night's dinner or whatever It was finding its way back up.

Head pounding, stomach jumping, I leaned over the kitchen sink and gave every inch of the contents of my stomach and then some to the drain.

"Ugh, god. I will never drink again if you take this feeling away." I uttered as I continued to throw up. "DAMN," I said holding my head. The sight of the vomit in the sink was enough to turn my stomach, but there was no way I could clean it up, not right at this moment so I slowly crept my way to my bedroom. Feeling a little better I sprawled my body across the bed. Looking over at my nightstand at

42

the clock, "shit, 9 o'clock, I swear to god I'm not feeling this shit, not this morning."

I reached for my cell phone to give to call Val and see if should handle the business today, my head was pounding and needed to recoup from the empty bottle of everclear I noticed on the floor on my way to my room. Today wasn't the day. I hated myself for allowing, Eureka and JC get into my feelings.

Picking up my cell phone, I noticed the blinking notification light.

I pressed the button, there were about 15 missed calls and several text messages. Some were from Val and the others were from JC.

Chapter 5

The real her.....

"Eureka what are you doing? I swear if you have messed up this deal for me." I yelled to the top of my lungs after I heard Tori's message. I didn't know whether to go over there or just let her back out of this Miami trip. The more I sat there seething with anger at Eureka's antics, I was nervous as hell. There is something about Tori that I need and feel I can't live without, now this stunt Eureka pulled may have caused me a future with Tori.

"What do you mean JC? What deal? Why are you so mad? I heard she was a good rep from a few of my modeling colleagues and I wanted to try her agency out. You and her have something going on that I should know about?"

"Eureka, cut he bullshit. You and I both know we are not, I repeat not in a relationship. We are as we both agreed friends with benefits."

She crossed her arms in front of her like a pouting child, "JC what if I want more now? We are both at a point in our lives that we can settle down and have a few littles ones, just look at us, our children will be pretty as ever. Come on aren't you ready?"

I thought about what she said for a moment, but not in the way she thinks. Yes, I am ready to settle down and maybe even start a family, but there is no way it would have been with her. Eureka had the sex appeal and career drive, but she lacked what I look for in a partner, substance, and depth. Although she was intelligent to her business, but she wasn't toward our business. See she was

45

shallow and tried to hide it from me, but even a blind man could see she was solely into herself. If she cuffed me I would only be a means to meet her end. Hell, even our children would serve a purpose.

A person with a drive is good, but only if it will serve someone or something other than themselves.

I have lived that fast life but I worked hard to get it, and there is no way I would let a beautiful gold digger take it all from me.

"Look Eureka, I swear you have issues, back when I wanted a real relationship with you, you put me on hold and made sure I knew it. Yes, I do want to settle down, but not with you."

I could see my words hit her in the heart and for the first time her jealous streak came to the surface and hard, "so what, you want that fat cow? I mean for real, you really want to be with someone who can fit a whole curtain around her waist and call it a skirt." She started laughing, but nothing she said I saw no humor in it.

I started clapping my hands as if to give her an applause. "Yes, that's it right there, the real Eureka. Now you say I want to be with a fat cow? Well no I don't want to be with a fat cow, in fact, I would love to be with a voluptuous, curvevaciousness, thick, cushion for the pushin', sexy woman. One who knows she is fine as hell no matter the size. Eureka just because a woman is not a size 0 doesn't make her ugly or even fat. See beauty is only skin deep, but ugly can be wrapped in a pretty package, but ugly to the bone." I looked her up and down as I walked over to check my voice mail one more time. I wanted and needed to talk with Tori. To fix anything Eureka may have wrecked.

Eureka walked behind me and snaked her arms around my waist, "come on baby, I'm sorry. It's just that we have been sexing each other for years and I thought it was time to step our game up, you know give the public what they want. Ya know that lil blue Ivy, instead we could cal her Jereka or JC Jr. It would be a good fit for both of our careers." I snatched away from her and spun around quickly like the devil himself came and took over me, "LEAVE! Get out now! See that's the shallow shit I'm talking about. I want to have my babies with someone who will love them, not use them as a meal ticket to further her career."

"But Jon-"

"Leave, and I don't want to have thing else to do with you, Eureka."

48

I walked over to my front door and opened it for her. She held her head down and walked out before she could turn around I slammed the door.

"FUCK YOU JON'TE, You can have that fat bitch. Any man would want me."

She stood outside my door yelling and kicking on it. I didn't say a word, instead I went over and called down to the front desk to have security come and take her out of the building. Once they removed her she was placed on a do not enter the list, she couldn't ever come into the building unless they could prove she was invited. They took her pictures and posted it in the security room, on what they called the 'wall of shame.'

The head of security called me down there and showed me the picture, he went over to their mini fridge and grabbed a couple of beers, "damn JC." he said as we cracked a beer open. Rex was with

49

the building for over ten years, so he was like part
of the family.

"JC what did you do to this one? She was wild,
pretty, but wild. I'd never seen Eureka like that the
whole time you were with her."

I shook my head from side to side as I held her
snapshot in my hand. Her make-up was smeared
and tears ran down her face. I felt a little sorry at
first because I think she did in her own way have
some type of feelings for me. But I wasn't feeling
her, not on that level.

"I don't know Rex, she wanted more than I could
give her." We took a swig of the beers.

"Yeah, well I'ma say this JC you are a good dude.
Rich, smart, and the females love you, so you must
get Midas touch." We both laughed.

"But for real JC be careful, I have seen vipers like her before. Sexy, pretty and dangerous. I would hate to see your picture on the news, where she done burnt all yo shit up and you right along with them."

I chuckled lightly as I thought about what he was saying. Eureka was becoming real clingy, but I really don't think she would do something stupid to ruin her career, it means too much to her.

I shrugged my shoulders and finished the beer. I thanked Rex then got up and went back to my apartment. I sat down and my cellphone rang, I took a deep breath, picked it up and looked the screen. I smiled when I saw who it was that was calling me. I took a deeper breath and prayed that she was still going to go on the trip with me.

"Hello, Tori I'm so glad you called

."

Chapter 6

The smiles on the outside can hide...

I sat going over spreadsheets and counting every dime D's ire's has made in the last year and it all came back the same, we were almost broke. There was no way I could take out another loan, the bank wasn't havin' that. I pondered on not going to Miami this week, but the truth was staring me in the face I needed to.

The connections JC had with the industry, could be very lucrative for my company and maybe even pull me out of this financial hole I'm stuck in.

"So what's the verdict? We going or what?" Val asked as she sat at the front of my desk.

"We have no other choice, we have to, we need some more clients and assignments for our models if not we will be bankrupt by the end of the year. Damn I wish like hell I didn't have to." I sighed a little more thinking about the visit from Eureka, and her revelations to me about the man I was now falling for.

I fought hard not to, but the more I tried the harder it became. I was in love with JC. The way we sexed was superb, but it was beyond that. Afterward, he would hold me in his arms as if he was holding on to dear life. I would sometimes fall asleep but could feel him planting kisses on my forehead. The moment I feel his loving touch I would pretend to stir in my sleep and move out of his arms.

But I found myself thinking about him more and more.

"I wished you would have let me handle that Heffa when she came in here the other day. Oh her pretty ass would have been messed up messing around with me." Val and I laughed at her, she was always in go mode, ready to fight.

"No Val that would have been playing right in her hands. I knew from the moment she walked in, that she had something on her mind, and something tells me all is not great in paradise as she claimed it to be. Look at this." I held up my cell phone so that Val could see my call log,

"Damn 50 missed calls! Damn what you got on this man, voodoo?"

I smiled knowing that I was being persuade like an animal in search of its prey. I finally called JC back last night and told him I would be accompanying him to Miami , but as far as something going on with him and I , that was dead, all the way now. Even if before I thought about hooking up with him, after Eureka's visit that was done. He tried explaining and apologizing, but I felt it best not to go any further.

"He heard my drunk voicemail I'd left him that night and begged me to come on the trip, and he was right our business does need the money and publicity. Hell, the fact that his lil dip wanted to stake her claim in him was enough for me to keep it business only. I don't have time for the drama, or looking stupid out here fight over a man."

"Shield, a man is not what JC is, he's a fuckin god! And you should want all of that. I know the sex is off the meter right? Girl yo ass got a blessing in your face and you gonna let it go? Well hell you lucky I don't do the sharing thing, cause baby I would get low ... get low... get low ooo www."

I laughed so hard watching Val dance around like a stripper and dropping low to the ground almost hard to come back up until tears were coming from my eyes.

"I needed that, I swear; you always know how to make me laugh."

"Laugh? No bitch I'm for real... shiddd." Val snapped her fingers to an imaginary beat and pranced out of my office into her's.

I put my head back down toward the huge piles of papers and spreadsheets on my desk. I heard a light knock at my door,

"What now Val, let me get some work done before we don't have a bus-"

57

I was caught off guard as I watched a disheveled Eureka standing in my doorway.

She had make-up kind of smeared on and her clothes were ripped. She looked like she'd been crying.

"Whats wrong, come in have a seat," I said as I got up from my desk and offered her a seat.

She paused for the moment looking me up and down then walked over to the chair I'd offered to her. Brushing her disheveled hair out of her face, she crossed her arms across her torn shirt, "I'm sorry to come here lookin less than professional, but I am really in need of this modeling job in Miami, JC and I are no more." She broke down crying. I had some compassion for her, I am a woman and there is an unspoken sisterhood code. I passed her some tissues. She wiped her nose and eyes and began looking at me with pleading eyes.

58

Her chest began to heave and in down rapidly as if she was struggling to get the words out.

"He... he..."

"It's okay take your time."

"He beat me," She said as she broke down in the chair.

I was shocked and confused. The JC I know would never put his hand on a female, much less even raise his voice. I studied her for a second, trying to find any hint of lies coming from her story.

"No are yo serious, why would he do that? He seems like a good guy judging the photos and stories that have been written about him."

She calmed herself and began to tell me about the night, I heard her say he got mad at her because of what another female told him, she never said the

59

name but I knew all too well who the female was that she spoke of. But for him to go this far, I really didn't see that.

"Look, I went over the list and there is no room for you to go to Miami, but there is a spot for you for our photo shoot in England." Her head spun around like she was possessed.

"Fuck you mean! First you steal my man, you fat bitch. Yeah I knew exactly who you were, Tori. I know JC is mine and nothing you do will keep him. Fat bitches like you need to stay in your fuckin weight class, and in your case that's the heavy weights." She stared laughing, like she just heard a joke, I could clearly see she was unraveling, fast.

Val rushed in my office, "Tori, whats going on?" she said sticking her head in the door.

"Oh I see fat bitches roll together, you nasty fat bitches do what yall do best, find an all-night buffet and eat."

Val looked at Eureka quickly and wrapped her hands around her neck. It took everything I had in me to get her off her Eureka.

"Val, Val... let her go she is not worth it."

"Fuck that! She can't come up in here talkin' cash shit and expect to not get the hands put on her. Ole skinny bitch. Yeah, I big but sexy and yes like my girl here will take your man."

Val was screaming at the top of her lungs trying to get to Eureka again. I turned to Eureka, "you need to leave, before I let her finish the job, and as for me stealing your man, well, all I can say is if he was happy with you then there would be no me. Now I suggest you take your business and gripe

61

somewhere else. As a matter of fact drop in our complaint box when you leave." She looked over the wall and the next thing out of her mouth proved just how dense she was,

"But I don't see your complaint box, you don't have one."

I shook my head from side to the side laughing at how dumb she could be, "exactly, now get out now before I call the police."

Eureka ran out of the door so fast that she left a piece of paper on the chair. I picked it up after I calmed Val down and she went back to her office for some coffee. I started reading the paper, now I was stuck once again, I knew I had to tell JC, there was no way but I shouldn't be the one to break some news like this to him. I know in my heart of hearts the lies she is running around town telling on him can destroy his career, but what on this paper can destroy the rest of his life.

Chapter 7

Ain't no fun when the rabbit got the gun...?

I rush and got inside of my black on black Mercedes
S-class, with the chrome rims and low profile tires.

I settled in the seat with all smiles. There was no
way I was giving JC up without a fight. I knowing
left a piece of paper on the seat. Tori was just like
any other female who has tried to come between
me and JC, and just like them, she will soon find
out what it is to take on a bitch like.

The word bitch to some is derogatory, but just like
the book 'who you callin a bitch' by urban novelist
Eureka, I'ma show and prove why anyone would
refer to me as the bitch.

I drove down Martin Luther King Boulevard in hopes of finding JC's car, and just like I thought, he was parked right outside of the 'Fiegous' night club, he takes all of his potential clients there and there a lot of paparazzi hang out hoping to get pictures of celebrities, knowing him I would have time to go home and get dressed up in my sexy attire. I want to give him an eye full of what he might miss. I pressed the gas on my car and made it to my house in less than ten minutes. I wasted no time getting out of the car, up the stairs, and into my apartment.

I rushed into my lavish walk-in closet and grabbed a sexy Dolce & Gabbana, barely there dress with a pair of matching Manolo Blahnik pumps. I literally ran in the bathroom and took a quick shower and got dressed. I pinned my hair up in a sexy fall ponytail, along with a pair of my hoop earrings with the matching necklace. I made sure I spray a touch of Dior perfume all over my body   especially on the front of my thong panties. I had plans to destroy and punish JC for ever thinking he could replace me and with a downgrade at that.

I gave myself a once over then rushed out of the house. I hit the alarm on my car, unlocked the door and got in. I pressed my playlist on the radio and searched for the song that described my moment,

"Wanna bumble wit the Bee hah?

Buzz, throw a hex on a whole family, dressed in all black like 'The Omen'

Have your friends singin' this is for my homey"

I turned the volume all the way up and bobbed my head to the beat. Lil Kim's part in this song always got me amped.

I drove down to the club reminiscing on the words I had to grow up by,

Fix your clothes, comb your hair, sit up straight, and don't eat so much nobody wants a fat girl.' My mother's words pierced my soul. All of my life I was taught if you were fat you weren't pretty and that no good man worth a damn will I want you if your looks are jacked up.

When I got in the modeling business I was turn on to some real self-hatred, I watched woman and men scrambled around like animals to get approval from society. I would go on many photo shoots some even told me I was too heavy, at a waist size of zero. I became part of the crazy when I developed an eating disorder, Bulimia, that's when I would eat everything I wanted then take my finger and make myself vomit it all up. For years I suffered in silence, until I meet Carl, JC cousin. He was kind and sweet and even helped me a lot when I was in training to sell real-estate all while I pursued a modeling career. I no longer felt like I needed to hurt myself to fit in, all because Carl showed me he worshipped me no matter what.

When Carl and I were about to get married, I found out he had a double life, one day Carl forgot his briefcase, so JC and I tried to catch up to him to give it to him. I called, but his phone was in the briefcase. When I spotted his car a few blocks ahead of us and told him to follow Carl's car. We pulled up on this secluded street and Carl drove his car in the garage. We blew the horn, but he didn't hear us and closed the garage door. I was confused because I didn't know whose house this was, and the fact that Carl was rushing there had me stuck.

I got out of the car after a few minutes JC and I were confused we thought how he could not have heard the horn, so I thought maybe he was going inside to introduce himself to the client. Then the other thought came to me was he was cheating? I'd had enough thinking and speculating, if he was cheating, whoever it was; they were about to meet me, his fiancé.

I slowly got out of the car after JC convinced me to knock on the door. Nerves all over the place but curiosity was getting the better of me, I walked up to the porch and rang the bell. A young man answered the door, he looked to be in his late twenties "hello may I help you?" The attractive young guy said as he opened the door.

"Bae, who is it, I know like hell it ain't Kar-" Carl walked to the door in a different outfit then he left out of our house with. His mouth gaped wide open as he stared at me and JC standing in the doorway. There were no words he could say.

69

With one side of my lip curled in disgust, "what the hell is this? Carl! And why in the hell are you dressed like this?"

"Carie, babe who is this? The guy said as confused as I was.

Carl rushed and slammed the door in my face. I beat on the door hard almost till my fist began to bleed.

"Come on Eureka, he is not gonna open the door." JC wrapped his arms around me and pulled me from the door broken and bruised. I was beyond shock, Carl never showed any signs of him being gay. But there it was in my face. He was two people that was the day my world came crashing down around me was the day I discovered Carl was, in fact, living a secret life as Carie.

I tried to get myself together somehow pick up the pieces, but I couldn't. JC was just as hurt because he loved his cousin and looked up to him. I guess in the midst of our sadness, two broken souls clung to each other and found, or at least I found my reason to go forward.

"Friends with perks my ass," I said aloud as I came up toward the block where the club sat. I parked in a small garage adjacent to the club, I didn't want JC seeing my car before I got inside. The show I had planned for him to see was going to be epic, and knowing by now that fat bitch Tori has told him what was on the paper if not she sure will, I know how simple minded females work.

"Everybody in the club getting' tipsy... (Er'body in da club getting tipsy) the music was off the chain, blaring through the speakers as I walked in the club
71

looking sexier than a cover model. Flashes of light came from all directions as camera took all of the celebrities that were entering the club pictures. I walked right up to the door past the mass crowd waiting to get inside. A few of the paparazzi, as we call them yelled for me to pose, I smile and waved. Walking towards the VIP section where JC and a few of his friends sat, I began snapping my fingers to the beat. I found the first booth and sat down making sure I could keep an eye on JC.

"Get me a bottle of your best champagne, and send one over to the table where the gentlemen are sitting."

"Any specific kind mama?" the waiter asked as I kept a skillful eye on JC, Joshua and LA Quentin.

"Yes, a bottle of Dom, nothing but the best for this night."

He hastily walked off and retrieved the bottles. I sat back in the plush booth and watched as JC and his friend's laughed and joked, he hadn't even noticed I was in the section. His usual winning smile and sexy swag were on a high tonight. Sitting next to him was one of his major clients, the next up and coming star in the basketball world, JohnL 'Cobo' Jefferson. Cobo was draped in long platinum chains and Tru Religion jeans and a pair of expensive sneakers. The club normally didn't allow jeans and gym shoes but for their celebrity clientele it was accepted. His six feet tall frame was sexy and I didn't mind getting up close and personal wit him.

Watching the waiter place the champagne I ordered for JC I sipped slowly. Cobo spotted me. I pretended not to see him as he walked over to my table.

73

"Hey, pretty lady, what you over here doin all by yo self? I tell you what how about me and you take this to a private room." He stood there with cockiness and full of arrogance. I looked him up and down ready to put him and all of his finesse in its place, but I decided to play it smooth, he was part of the plan to get back at JC.

Instead, I smiled, "well nice to meet you and you are?"

"Pretty lady, stop playing you know good and well who I am."

I extend my hand out for a shake, "no, I don't, but you are sexy as hell tho."

I didn't want to seem too cocky and not stroke his ego. Men are all the same a little bit of worshipping goes a long way.

74

"No I really don't but I would love to get to know you tho."

He chuckled and sat down next to me and wrapped his arms around my shoulders.

"Real aggressive and straight forward I see," I said as I moved over slightly giving him enough room to get comfortable.

After I stroked his ego a bit, he loosened up then the show began. He talked about himself and all this money he has and I laughed loudly and played with Cobo under the table. I allowed him to touch the kitty and kiss my neck. Bottle after bottle he drank until he was wasted to the point he couldn't stand up straight.

"Co...me on lesh...ta...this to my room." He said standing up slurring his words. I pretended to be drunk and stumbled to stand with him.

75

"Wait, wa...it a minute let me go to the ladies room." Acting as if I was stumbling drunk, I noticed I'd gotten JC attention. I went right in the direction of the bathroom until I got to a side exit door. I opened the door slightly to let in one of the paparazzi, "look just like we discussed, and make your way over there." I said pointing towards the VIP section. "Make sure you get a real good shot." The thirsty photographer nodded in agreement as he discreetly came in the door.

I went it to the bathroom to make it all look legit. I came out and pretended to stumble back over to Cobo, "oh I'm sorry." I said as I fell on top of him.

"That cool lil momma. Now let's get this party crackin." Cobo kissed me so hard I almost slapped the taste from his mouth. Instead I pulled back and whispered in his ear.

"You want this pussy? Take it then." Just like I suspected he grabbed my arm and pulled me. It was time for the show. I pulled away from him and he pulled me back to him, "come on lil momma, you said if I want it I can take it. So stop frontin' I want it and you gon give it." The smell of alcohol and weed coming from his breath would have gotten me hot on any other night, but not tonight, tonight he was about to be a big pawn in my game.

"No Cobo, stop. I just want to go home." I said loud enough to get JC's attention.

Being the man JC is I knew he wasn't going to allow this so I put in a little extra tear or two,

"Cobo I said I wanna go home, just leave." Cobo continued to pull on me because I told him I loved to role play.

77

"Come here you lil freaky bitch, you gon give me that pussy."

I pulled my arm away again this time so hard I fell to the floor. When I was about to stand up a firm familiar hand was helping me up from the floor. Once I could stand, I leaped into his arms, "thank you JC, and thank you. I don't know what got into him." And right on cue the camera flashed taking our embracing moment. Inside I was too happy this couldn't have played out any better if I'd written a script.

"You can have that crazy muthafucka," He said as he walked to the other side of the room where tons of groupies waited their turn to get a piece of him.

"Are you okay Eureka?" JC asked as he helped me to a seat.

78

I played the role a little more and broke down with tears and all. I wanted him to take me home with him, but the pictures the photographer took were all I needed.

"Yes I'm fine, I just want to go home. Thank you JC, I know I didn't take us ending things to well but I thank you for being a friend even after the way I acted." I stood and gave him one final hug with a kiss on the cheek making sure the camera got it all.

He asked the bouncer to make sure I made it safe to my car. When I got inside after playing the role of a lifetime, I was pleased with myself. Everything I wanted was going to be mine.

Chapter 8

Just be a man about it...

Sitting in my office with my thoughts all over the place. Should I tell JC what was on that paper Eureka dropped. I would dial his number, on the first ring I would hang up. Then I thought of finding him and putting the paper in his hand and letting the chips fall where they may.

 I was about to call one more time until I heard the front door chime open. I looked up and JC was walking right into my office. I hung my desk phone up. One mind was telling me just pass him that paper and be done with him, Eureka and any of her antics she brought with her and him. But seeing his eyes and the smile adorned on his face, I had second thoughts.

"Hello stranger." He said in a sexy deep voice.

"Well hello to you to sir." I said smiling from ear to ear. I was the power he led over me. Whenever I would come face to face with him all I could see was him, nothing and no one but him. I was in deep. The more I fought it the deeper I fell.

He walked over and stood right in front of me. His cologne and a hint of alcohol invaded my space. But I welcomed it, the intoxicating aroma was one that I longed for since we last touched.

He stepped so close that not even air could separate us, "Tori." He said rubbing the top of my hand.

"I want you. Please I need you." I parted my lips to answer, but was immediately silenced as his tongue entered my mouth. I tried to faintly resist

81

him, but couldn't. I wanted and needed him at this moment. Nothing mattered but him and me.

I gave into my passion an explored his mouth with my tongue.

He leaned me back on my desk. I stopped and turned quickly to push the pile of papers on my desk to the floor.

He immediately grabbed me around my waist and kissed me again. My body was pressed against the desk as his hands hungrily traced my thick thighs and hefty breast. Caressing them gently, he gave each of them special attention as if it was a meal of the gods. Nibbling on my nipples through my shirt, as he slowly unbuttoned it; without missing a moment to kiss my lips.

The thickness and fullness of his lips were so soft and firm. He stroked and pulled at my skirt, abruptly stopping he looked me in my eyes and said, "if this is too much let me kn-".

Before he could finish speaking, I stopped him with a kiss. We tasted each other, losing ourselves in the moment, he lowered his body to face my pelvic. Looking up at me he slowly removed my skirt. He was a master of strategically removing my skirt from around my thick hips. I could see the lust and a hint of love in his eyes. I couldn't explain it, but he made me feel like I was the most beautiful woman he'd ever laid eyes on; to have me would be the blessing he'd prayed for.

As my skirt fell to the floor and I could see his manhood was erect. He stood up in front of me, but unlike him I hungered for him. I eagerly unbuttoned his belt then his Imani pants. When his pants hit the floor, the front of his Sean John boxer shorts extended to the desk almost touching my pussy hood; all of his fully erect 10 inch penis was ready.

We kissed again, then he lowered himself back in front of me and began nibbling at my honeypot through my Lane Bryant intimate collection lace panties. He nibbled and licked until he began removing them with his teeth. He laid me on top of the desk. I spread wide for him to see my clean shaven kitty. Every spa day, I would ask for a special trim on the hairs on my honey pot, a long trail and arrow at the end pointing to my clit. Briefly He gave me a coy smile then took the tip of his tongue tracing the top of my kitty until he placed it right on my clit.

"Mmm...mmm" his muffled sound filled the room as he sucked and devoured every inch of my swollen clit. His touch immediately had me releasing my nectar all over his face. The more I released the more sounds of him licking, sucking, and slurping between my thighs on his favorite meal. Our passionate moans were so loud that we didn't hear out phones ringing. There was no way he was stopping, and no way was I going to let him.

He sucked my clit and a rapid pace the slowed down to kiss and pull at it as if he was writing a note or symphony across it. I wanted to taste him inside of my mouth. I nudged him to ease up so that I could make him feel as good as I did. Instead, he made sure I was spread eagle on the desk and he placed his body on top of me upside down.

His ten inches of pleasure was in my face. I eased it into my wet waiting mouth.

Taking his manhood deep inside of my mouth, I could feel the tip touching my tonsils, I began to gag a little as the tip of my tongue touched the

85

top of his scrotum sack. I bobbed up and down as the mix of saliva and pre-cum filled my mouth.

Licking and sucking, pulling and nibbling I devoured his manhood as if I was on an audition for the next top porn star.

Never had a man handle my body like I was a small girl.

He placed my legs around the top of his head as we were in a sixty –nine position, spreading my ass cheeks apart as he plunged his tongue in and out of my anus. I was wide open, his personal playground. He took turns licking my clit, then to my anus in a rapid but steady motion then He rolled me over to the top of him; with pussy right in his mouth he positioned me directly on top of his face.

I thought I was going to smother him with all of these thighs so I tried easing up to make sure he had air, but he grabbed me closer and continued to feast on my swollen clit as I sucked on his penis. He felt my body tensing up as he rapidly flicked his tongue on my kitty, with each stroked my kitty creamed.

With one long, strong flick of his tongue I released a flow of honey that seemed endless, "OH GOD, YES! YES! YES!" Sounds of our passion echoed throughout the entire office. I clenched my thighs together to get a little relief from this lovely assault, but no win, his head game was official and I loved it. "Ple...ple...please, baby." My pleas fell on deaf ears as he continued to pull, suck, lick and slurp every inch of my kitty. I was so into it I couldn't even finish giving him head.

He quickly got up and slammed his long hard manhood inside of my throbbing kitty. I loved it when he handled me. The motion was fast and the pounding was steady. Place each of my legs on each of his arms, he pulled me to the edge of the desk. With my ass cheeks hanging partially off of the desk, he thrust his hips deeper, winning in a circular motion making sure he filled every inch of my hole. Holding my legs wide and out to each side in a v like position, he wedged himself deeper between my thighs.

"Damn, Tori baby... you got some goo- oh my fuckin god. Girl, sll shit, marry me. SHIT! Let me put a ring on it." He was like a wild man, his pace sped up and his thrusting was deeper. It was so good, "YES, YES, FUCK YES!" I screamed out. Caught in the heat of the moment I don't think either of us was thinking about what we were asking.

We sexed each other for what seemed like hours until our bodies began to convulse as we simultaneously released our nectar.

The feeling of bliss and euphoria was the mood, and nothing else mattered not even the note and the headache, Eureka will bring with her. He collapsed on top of me, exhausted and panting trying to catch our breath as our bodies lay in a weird position, half of me hung off the desk and he still had my legs in the v shape position.

He kissed my stomach and breast for a moment. No words were spoken, it was clear to me I am in love and it felt good.

Chapter 9

All seems right in Paradise

For the next week, we'd had a wonderful time. No Eureka not a peep and that was odd but welcomed. Tori and I were on a new level and I was right I loved her and now I know there is no denying she loves me. I made the arrangements for the hotel to have mine and Tori's room adjoining. We were going to get some work done and make it at least look professional for the most part.

We flew first class, our plane ride was pleasant full of laughter and talk. I introduced Tori to a few of my colleagues that were also coming, so they could fill up their cliental roster.

"So tell me a little bit about yourself Tori." One of my co- workers said as he brought her a glass of wine.

Tori began to talk about her agency like she should unaware that Mr. Slick was calling himself trying to flirt.

"Oh so you're not married? Wow that's shocking a beautiful woman such as yourself should be the first on the list. Well let's see if we can change that when we get to Miami." She laughed as she noticed my facial expression. Her business partner Val chimed in to lighten the mood, "im not married either, so I guess it will be a double wedding, because there is no way she is getting married before me." We all busted out laughing.

"Please return to your seats, as we prepare to land in Miami International. We would love to thank you for flying Montel airlines were your pleasure, is our

91

business." The perky flight attendant announced over the PA system.

There were two black limos waiting for us one was for Tori and her staff, and the other was for myself and colleagues. We arrived at the hotel and checked in. everyone got their room numbers and keys. I made sure Tori's room and mine were on the end of the hall away from everyone.

"Well hello. Mr Cullbirth." Tori's soft voice spoke from the other room.

"Hello to you Ms. Tori Williams."

Tori stepped in my room. Just as we were about to embrace there was a knock at the door.

92

"Who is it?" I yelled out.

"Hotel messenger service."

"Okay, I will be right there."

Tori stood for a second until she heard a knock from her room door. She went back in her room to answer her door as I did mine.

I opened the door and there stood a young man with a balloon and big blue bouquet of carnations.

"Jon 'Te Cullbirth?" he asked.

"Yes, but im sure you have the wrong room, these couldn't possibly be for me."

He passed me an envelope along with the flowers and balloon that read 'congratulations.' I opened the note and there was a small note 'We're having a baby!' With all my love Eureka.

93

I dropped the flowers and the blue and silver balloon from my hands as the word from the letter were caught in my throat. Just as I was about to rush over to Tori and share this horrible news, she was standing in the door way of our adjoining rooms with a newspaper in her hand.

Trembling with tears streaming down her face, she looked as if the life was just sucked right out of her.

She held the paper out ward to me. I had forgotten about the note I held in my hand.

There were photos from the night Eureka and Cobo were at the club, with the headline, 'it's official she said yes!" I read the article underneath the picture of me helping her from the floor and she planted a kiss on my cheek. It did seem like we were in and embrace, but she and I both knew that wasn't the case. The article said that sources close to JC and Eureka have confirmed they are the new

94

power couple are in fact about to be married and a small surprise is on the way.

Before I could say a word Tori slammed the door and locked it.

Standing there confused and hurt, because I know this lie has hurt Tori. I knew she would never believe me now that these pictures are in the open and this lab test showing Eureka was pregnant, any and all hope I had for a future with Tori was gone.

Chapter 10

No happy Endings

JC beat down the door all day and part of the night. He slid a few I'm sorry notes under the door but I wasn't trying to hear that. There was no way I could pursue anything with him. Eureka won. She wanted him now she has him but where does that leave me? Alone and hurt.

Val sat at the foot of my bed in silence, not really knowing the right words to say. For the first time in our 20 year sisterhood she was speechless.

"Come on Tori you have to eat something."

"No Val Im okay. I can't really eat can't sleep. I just want to leave and go home."

Val rubbed my shoulder as she came up to the top of the bed and sat next to me, "look sis, I know this is hard and I really can't find the right words to tell you , but what I do know you are strong and full of faith. All of this will work itself out. Now come on get dressed we have a meeting in the conference room with a few of the new clients. We still have to make money honey."

I somehow managed to sit up for the first time since last night. To say I was broken would be an understatement. For the first time in a long time I'd given myself to what I was always told I couldn't have, and just like that it was all gone.

"Okay you are right, let me get dressed and I will meet you down stairs."

"You sure? I could wait on you."

"No im sure, I have to somehow get up and get moving."

Val kissed my forehead and reluctantly left the room.

I stood up in the mirror as I unpacked a nice simple outfit to put on. I felt tears wailing up and quickly went to the shower, there I could cry my heart out and allow the water to wash the tears away down the drain. Thirty minutes later I was out of the shower and in my room sitting parched on the side of the bed; still in a daze and somewhat confused. I thought about how I would react when I see his face, would I scream at him or would I embarrass myself by breaking down in tears in front of everyone?

So many thoughts. I looked over to the floor where our rooms were joined to see yet another note.

This time I picked it up and it was a little longer than the others.

'Tori, words can even began to tell you how sorry I am, for all of the pain I caused you and now I feel. I really wished we could have had that life together. That day I asked you to marry me, it wasn't because of the sex or the fact it made me feel food, but it was real. I want you and I want to marry you. Baby my heart is broken and I don't expect you to just believe me because as they say a picture is worth a thousand words, but trust me when I tell you those pictures were real but not with the bullshit article that was written along with them. The same time you got those pictures, I got a lab confirmation that Eureka is carrying my child. FUCk! No I am not happy with this, but it is all my fault. I should have ended things with her a long

99

time ago. She set this up to a tee and I have a

feeling it will only get worse and I will not expose

you to her and this circus.

Please know that I love you, yes you, and I will

never stop. I decided to leave and go back home. I

couldn't bare looking at you and not touch or talk

to you. Girl you have rocked me to the core and I

am man enough to admit it, im whipped. I hope in

the near future you can forgive me or at least be

my friend. If I can only have that part of you in my

life I would still be blessed.

Forever yours,

Jon 'Te

Tears soaked the letter as I dropped it in my lap. I
wanted to at least see him before he left. To me
that was a coward's move face me like a man. Own
up to it, look at the hurt he caused. But on the

other hand I understood, Eureka was really a mess and the fact she s is having his baby will only make things worse. There would be no happy ending no us.

Chapter 11

One Big Happy

"Baby hurry we gonna be late," I called out to JC from the other room. He was so mad with me because of the baby and how the pictures found their way into the newspaper that was months ago. Once he got the confirmation that I was indeed pregnant he asked me to move in with him. That fat cow was no more. I heard she moved overseas somewhere. Good for her big ass now I can have my man.

"Ouch, this damn baby." I was happy that I had him and I guess pains and having my perfect figure stretched all out of place was the price I had to pay. I was ending my second trimester and things were falling right in place. JC heart was broken and all settled down with our new family and me. I found out in through an ultrasound that I was carrying a bouncing baby boy and he was doing wonders for my hair, nails, and skin, now Vijay-jay is another story. JC hadn't touched me in months and I needed some pole of joy badly. Every time I would get him to a point where he would touch me something happened where he stops. But no matter I will have him again, mind, body, heart, and soul.

102

"What time is your appointment, I need to make a few calls first then we can go." He quickly came in my room and walked back out before I could answer.

I held my stomach and had a talk with my son, "look baby boy daddy will come around."

I stood up to walk in the bathroom and a hard sharp pain surged through my entire body, followed by sharp constant cramps around my pelvic area.

"JC! Jont'te!" I screamed. He came rushing in the room. The expression on his face let me knew it was far worse than I suspected. I watched his eye fixed on the floor, when I looked down I saw a huge amount of blood and what looked like water on the floor.

103

"Oh my God! HELP! My baby." JC rushed and called for an ambulance. While I sat in the mess that came from my body. The pain became more and more unbearable, I was in full blown labor. Everything in the room seemed like it started spinning and got blurry. I held my head as I tried to stand up and get my balance.

Waking up to a beeping sound and wires all over my stomach caused me to panic, I tried jumping up from the bed only to be restrained.

"What's going on? Where is my son." My voice cracked with fear and the dryness of my throat caused me to sound almost in auditable. JC stood by my side holding my hand with a worried expression.

"Calm down Reka, please let the doctors help our son." JC gently rubbed my hand as we both watched the monitor, the numbers on the screen seemed to go up then back down, and they went so low that the machine started beeping loudly.

"JC, what's wrong. Oh, my god. My son."

Doctors and nurses rushed in the room I heard one of them say, "we have got to get her up to the O.R. stat!" One nurse rushed over and moved JC to the side and injected something into my IV. I couldn't move. Everything went numb, my eyelids began to feel like sand bags. I could no longer keep them open. I remembered seeing JC warm smile and holding my hand.

Chapter 12

Some Secrets…. Need not be a secret

"Hey, you gonna tell him Tori? He deserves to know."

"No I am not, I'ma just sit here in England and live my life. Besides after what JC and Eureka went through how would it look me just springing this news on him? Look I am blessed and I will just enjoy my little blessing till the end of time."

"I know girl, it was tragic. They say JC was so hurt he went into a seclusion and Eureka, well let's say she was Eureka. Girl she had the nerve to prance around like the worst thing that could have happened to them didn't. I mean to lose your child, I couldn't even imagine. So how is my niece? I know she is big as ever."

"She is and I feel so complete. Val, I never knew I could love someone as much as I love this little girl. I see some much of him in her. Well, the part I remember. Anyway, let me let you get back to work. How is the business? I have a few models coming your way soon we need to continue to make De 'sire's top notch."

Val and I finished our conversation about the next month's schedule. It has been almost two years since I left and came over to set up our office in London, England.

I watched the news and read online news articles about JC my heart was crushed when I left, but I had to do what was best for him and me. After that trip to Miami, I found out that I was pregnant. I was going to tell him but heard that he'd moved Eureka in with him and that they were getting married, for real this time. Val being my good-

good girlfriend kept me holding it together. Many times I was going to break down and tell him, but I didn't want my child, our child to be hated and possibly even hurt by Eureka.

 When the news was released online about them losing their son, I decided it was best he never knew about Samya, our daughter.

"Mama, me wan some uice." My daughter came in my office running and jumping up in my lap. She was one and a half now and her speech was broken, but I understood all too well what she was saying.

"Ms. Mcullerton can you look in the mini fridge in the cafeteria and grab her an apple juice, please? And a fresh banana, I don't want her eating too much junk food before lunch."

"Sure thing mom. Come Lil lady lets's get you your juice box."

"No that's okay she can wait here with me while you get it, I want to spend some time with my princess."

The nanny walked out of the office. I started playing and cooing with Samya. She was getting bigger and more and more her features were undeniable, JC was defiantly her father.

"Come her lil white girl." I would call her because her skin was so bright like his. She had the shape of my eyes and the color of his. Her hair was curly much like his and her face was shaped just like his. The only resemblance she really held to me was her eyes everything else was him.

"Ms. Williams, London Black Post's photographer is on the line, he wants to know if he can schedule

109

you and appointment for the article?" My secretary chimed in from the intercom.

"Tell him I wil get back to them as soon as I can." I held the button down for a minute. I thought about taking those photos of me. They wanted to get an in-depth look at my life as a young African-American business owner here in England. There were only a few in the industry and D'sires was the one of the top up and coming modeling agencies here. I didn't really want to expose my private life, or allow pictures of my baby to the surface. Much like JC the spotlight is not where I wanted her to be.

"Ma-ma sad?" Samya asked rubbing my face with her soft little hands.

"No, mommy not sad little miss nosey." I tickled her stomach and she laughed so loud. The sound of her being happy and carefree was more than all I needed.

I kissed her forehead then pulled her close to my chest holding her close to my heart. Her puffy little rosy pink cheeks and light brown eyes had me memorized. At least I had a part of him. Although I never got that chance to explore a deeper love with him, but based off what I do know I doubt that I will ever stop loving him he will forever hold a key piece of my heart.

I continued to play and spend some time with Su, I gave the nanny the rest of the afternoon off. I took her to the park and taught her what every mother should teach her daughter no matter how young, shopping.

I walked in front of this stand-alone boutique, "mmm plus size lingerie." I read aloud wondering if I should go inside.

111

"A' have a look ." a deep toned voice with a British accent said. I turned and quickly looked him up and down, then curled one side of my lips.

"Do you make this a habit of talking to a stranger about their personal garments?"

He lightly laughed, "No, no mom I'm sorry if I came off that way. Believe me, love, I'm no pervert. Please allow me to introduce myself, I am Hennry." He reached out to shake my hand. I picked Samya up and walked inside of the store. I felt uneasy and wanted to get away fast.

Once I got inside of the store I sat her down in a chair to regain my composure, it was something about him. I couldn't put my finger on it, but something was off.

"Hello welcome to Dangles, home of the most luxurious and affordable and not to mention

112

sexiest intimate apparel for plus size women. How can I assist you today?" a perky sales clerk walked up to me, startling me as I tried to see where this Hennry person was at.

"Ooh-no, I'm sorry I just wanted to-" stopping in mid-sentence. I couldn't help it when I noticed a cream colored teddy with a guarder piece at the bottom the sides were v-shaped and gold or copper colored mesh material on the side.

"You know what, I want this. What sizes do you carry?"

"well mam, this is our new fall collection, Khandy' by one of our local designers. We have this up to a size 6x and special order if needed."

 I made sure Su was sitting there safe while I took a feel of this garment.

113

The softness of the material along with what felt like elastic made it one of the most exquisite I have ever felt.

"Did you say the designer of this was local?"

"Why yes, he is. His name is Hennry Scarbrough and He has a great eye for this, in fact, we carry a few more of his pieces." The sales person point along their walls where some of the sexiest intimate apparel sat. Much of them looked better than the Victoria secrets collection for a smaller woman. The way the colors flowed together, some bright yellow with a splash of mint green and some darker shades of purple trimmed in white lace. His eye was unlike most I'd seen.

The sales clerk showed me a business card of the designer and it was the same gentlemen that

114

approached me outside. I felt a little embarrassed that I'd overreacted like that.

I smiled and asked the sales clerk for one of every set. I had a good eye for fashion and I was sure this would put D'sires on a whole other level. Plus size models of all shapes, colors, and size. I wanted to run a whole campaign featuring his designs.

I went over and picked up Su and paid for my purchases. Making sure I held his business card close I was sure I'd be calling him real soon.

Samya and I finished our little mommy daughter shopping trip. For the rest of the day, my mind was on this next venture. I knew this would be the next biggest thing since sliced bread in the fashion industry.

The colors, freaky designs, along with the size options I knew it would be a hit.

115

Walking in my front door I was greeted with a huge box. I opened the second door and got Samya inside then I went back out and picked the box up. "Mm- this must be the clothes Val promised for Su. Hey, Sue baby your auntie got you some things." Called out as I carried the big box and put it on the floor. She waddled over beating on the box like a drum.

"No baby girl lets open it up and see what she bought you."

I struggled to get the top part open then I finally did. She sent her tons of clothes and a huge tricycle. The pink ribbons falling from the handlebars were all Samya wanted. I pulled everything out and Su immediately tried to ride her bike.

"Ma-ma, me wan."

"Later hunny bunny, let mommy clean this up okay." The note inside said, 'love you niece pooh.'

Valerie was my rock even miles away. The expression on Su's face was exactly the one JC made when he would smile.

"Damn, how am I gonna make it through this. Apart of me wants to call and let him know he has a daughter and the other half is not ready to share her, not with his evil wife. If she tries to do anything to my baby I will kill her ass.

117

Chapter 13

Settling for the ....

I felt guilty that we lost our son, the fact I stressed and longed for Tori must have made Eureka worry about getting me to love her and with the stress of it all, her body couldn't handle carrying our son full term.

Jont'te junior is the name we gave him. He lived all of seven days before he died.

I don't remember ever praying that hard to any god that would grant me my wish that my son would live. I would have made the deal with the devil himself just so that he would survive and I did just that, I married Eureka in the hospital chapel out of

118

guilt and remorse. Hoping it would save my son after the doctors told us he had a 50/50 chance of survival.

"Yes just put it down over there," I said to the movers as they helped bring things in my new office. Since the death of my son I choose to quit my job and go into seclusion that was until reality hit me , my new wife was acting like she'd gotten over the worst thing that could have happened fast. I slipped into a low place, Tori moved away and my son was dead, I didn't think I would ever be able to get out of the bed much less go on with my life. A year later almost to the date, here I am starting my own sports agency firm. From time to time, my mind and thoughts would fixate on Tori, us and what we could have had.

"Yo, yo JC you   the man…. What it do?"
119

"Man we thought we lost you for a minute. Nice office bruh." Joshua and Quentin came in loud as they plopped down on the couch next to the large window overlooking the city.

"Damn! How in the fuck did you cop this? Man JC I know you had some paper but damn boy, this here is official." Quentin expressed his excitement for my new accommodations.

"Yeah JC this shit is some real exclusive lookin shit. What you do rob a bank?"

"Shit, I wish, the fact is I had some chips stacked and the lawsuit I slapped the hospital with for the death of my son they decided to settle out of court. Yea even tho it wasn't their fault I did what most grieving parents do, look for someone to blame."

I couldn't help but wonder when I sued them was it the right way to go, but what's done was done.

120

"So how's the married life?" Quentin smirked.

"What are you smirking for? It is what it is." I shrugged my shoulders as I thought of my marriage and the horrible mistake I made.

"Damn, you don't seem too happy. I tell you what how about we go ahead and hit the club and do like we use to before all the fame, fortune, and marriage." We busted out laughing because Joshua knew too well there was no marriage for his self-proclaimed player of the year status.

I briefly reminisced about Tori, more so than often, lately I find myself thinking of her more and more. Since Val told me she left her to run the office over here and moved over to set up their England office, I thought it was best if I just let her go. But not without a price, I loved her and wished that everything could have turned out different.

121

"A yea lets go, I need a drink." I grabbed a few things. Getting ready to shut my laptop down, I noticed a notification from someone named Harrell Scarbrough. I opened the email and skimmed through it, I made a mental note to follow up with him on the next business day.

Nothing was odd, he stated he was looking for some representation on his new basketball career in the pros, he was an up and coming star out of England making his transition to the United States. I turned the lights off and closed the door on our way to the bar for a much-needed guy's night out.

Walking up to the club door I could hear 'There something in this liquor, the air is getting thicker. Can't help but to stare at you-oo, girl what did you do? To me... what did you put up in my cup girl-girl cause I want you.' Chris' Brown's new single could be heard on the outside of the doors it was so loud.

I walked over toward the bouncer, "JC my man. Long time no see, how ya been"

"Man Guape, I see you ain't lost no meal or the gym. Damn man, what are you lifting trees now?"

We laughed. He told me heard about the loss of my son and that he was sorry, but he was happy to see me back in the building.

Walking to the VIP section to seat at my usual table, I noticed a young lady dancing with about

123

two or three guys. She rocked and swayed to the beat barely holding her balance. She began dropping to her knees in front of them as the guys surrounded her almost in a semi- circle.

 I walked closer because I thought her dress looked familiar. I stepped up right in time, as Eureka dipped low. With a hazed look in her eyes, she glared at me with a smirk on her face and continued to sashay her ass across the front of one of the guy's pelvis.

 I wanted to slap the slob out her, but I noticed she was out of it, high off something. So I walked over and snatched her up from the floor and pulled her out of the club stammering and slurring her speech.

"FUCK YOU JC! MY SON... my son di- it's your fault. Had you just loved me and me only? But nooo,

124

noooo you pined over this fat bitch. Why? Huh...
Why? Was our son's life worth it?"

Her words hit me like a ton of bricks as I shoved her
in the passenger seat of my car. Cameras flashing
all over, but I had to get her out of there before she
did any more damage. I hurried in the driver's seat,
I didn't even have time to let my boys know I left.
My main concern was Eureka. Right no she is
hurting and clearly high on something.

"Look I know you don't mean what you are saying
now. I'ma just take you home and you can sleep
this off."

Don't tell me what the fuck I mean. You fuckin liar!
You married me and yet you still wanted her ass.
Tori has a part of you I will never have, not even
our dead son will have. Why JC? Why? Aren't I
pretty enough. See I got my body back, LOOK! Just
look at me, any man would love to have this." She
125

started squirming around in her seat pulling her dress overhead and stripped down to her bra and panties.

Then she began rubbing between her thighs, "I'm a sexy bitch, JC look at all this. I'm a sexy ass bitch." She unbuttoned her bra and tossed it out of the window.

"Eureka! What the hell are you doing?"

"Shut the fuck up, I'm enjoying life."

She leaned out of the window naked, her hair blowing in the wind and her breast flapped in the wind.

Swerving all over the road, I tried pulling her back in the car.

"Let me the fuck go, I have nothing left to live for. I have nothing! My son is dead, you don't love me ...

126

and this fat bitch ... that fat bitch Tori has the one thing I wanted by you, your child!"

I held her wrist tightly until she said that. I lost control of the car and skidded off the road into the construction site.

Chapter 14

Everything is not what it seems

A few months has passed and I am really beginning to feel Hennry. He has become a good friend. His whole demeanor is refreshing and welcomed. Since JC, I haven't had the heart or want to be in a relationship and mommy duties gets a little lonely some days, but I love my daughter.

"Hennry we have to interview a few of the plus-sized models for your new line-up tomorrow, will you be available to come by the office around noon?"

"Sure. I hope these are sexy, that last batch ... well, let's just say they were no you."

I smiled and blushed a little, flattered by the compliments. "but I'm no model love, I will leave that up to the sexy people."

He stood up and walked in front of me, His smile was bright, but the look in his eyes were filled with lust. He extended his hand for me to place mine inside of his, "come here, and walk with me." He led me to a large mirror. "Here put this on, I want to show you something."

I'd become so comfortable with him, that I didn't question. He gave me a bra and panty set from his upcoming collection. I got dressed in the bathroom.

When I came out, I had on the set. His mouth gaped open and his eyes fixed on my face. He quickly rushed over to the other side of the room, "here put these on and these." He passed me a pair of black Gucci pumps and a pearl necklace with matching earrings.

Here I stood in front of this long mirror in hot pink and gold with lilac colored roses on the front of the panties and the same design was on the bra. The snug, revealing fit of the panties were just right.

"40-42-36, I guessed it about right. Tori now this is sexy, your body is nothing to hide. I love every inch down to the dimples on your ass cheeks. See a big beautiful woman such as yourself needs to take pride in herself. Yes, a lot of women possess a certain beauty, but a BBW. Bold Beautiful women are what has been forgotten." He started snapping pictures of me. I felt so comfortable with his words that I allowed myself to fall into the moment. I began to seductively pose as he talked.

"My queen, you are what I want to represent my line. You. Not some stranger who has no

130

knowledge of how to embrace her sexiness. I mean own her body out right. Tori, you have that certain swag about you." He turned me around in a circle as he took a full view of my body.

Feeling a little nervous because of the extra weight I put on after having the baby, I tried to cover myself.

"No, no please don't hide. You are perfect. Tori your size only intensifies you, to me." He took my hand and raised my arm over my head to twirl me once more then he kissed me on the neck.

I jumped In more places than one. "Oh, I'm sorry, Tori if I over stepped my boundaries. I know you can feel by now that I am feeling you and my desire for you is more than sexual. But the way you embody everything I want in a woman …. Makes it harder for me to resist."

As my center got moist, I briefly entertained the thought of him and me exploring our physical attraction. I really began to feel him and all that he posed as well. His mocha skin, strong –well-toned abs, Almond shaped hazel eyes and the texture of his ceaser cut hair resembled the actor 'Lance Gross'.

Taking the tip of my finger, I traced the top of his shoulders. I hadn't had some lovin in almost two years and it was about time. Our lips touched allowing our tongues to explore each other's mouths.

He reached in back of me to unbutton my bra, "No JC, we can-." Realizing I called him JC I lowered my arms and tears began to fall as if it had started raining. I stepped back trying to cover up what was left of my pride and hurt.

"I am so sorry Hennry. I didn't mean to call you by my daughter's father's name. It's just that I haven't been intimate with anyone since he and I separated."

"Again, no need to apologize. I understand getting over someone you love is hard. Well, the understanding you both come to, which is labeled as love. It could take years, months or days to get over a broken relationship, no one has a full plan for us to just move on."

I heard a hint of sadness in his voice as he spoke words filled with wisdom.

"Peace Queen, we will table this until you are ready. I'm here as a friend whenever you need to talk."

Hennry walked over by the door he stopped briefly as if his mind drifted to something or someone.

133

I grabbed a robe laying on the chair and wrapped it around my body. Every part of me. Especially my honey pot wanted to call him back and indulge in some mind blowing sex, but I had to maintain myself. I had to once again deal with the fact I took a gamble on love but lost.

Chapter 15

I will do anything

"Look baby girl call me when you get this message. I'm starting to worry about you. I love you."

I left another voicemail for Eureka, for what seemed like the millionth time, and she still hasn't returned my calls. I needed her to know that I almost had Tori right where I wanted her and soon she will be out of her hair.

Eureka and I dated for years, long before that pretty boy JC got his hooks into her and destroyed my precious jewel. I would do anything for her. I am on the acting gig of a lifetime. I really deserve and Oscar for this role. Big girls have never been my forte, in fact, they really turn me off. Each time I had to visual a Nikki Minji or Ciara or one of them so I could muster up a stiff one when I looked at Tori.

When she first contacted me and told me about this idea to get Tori to fall for me I was dead set against it. Hearing the hurt and revenge in her voice, I thought on it. When I about to tell her no, because I really don't like big girls, she paid me a visit to seal the deal.

After sexing me until I couldn't see what was right from wrong Eureka and I came up with a better plan to get what we wanted. I wanted money and she wanted revenge.

I picked a photo of Tori wearing the two piece I gave her to try on the other day, although her face is pretty, but she had too much extra for my taste, really disgusting. Her big stomach and extra roll

136

just above her hips really made me want to vomit, but because of the deal and all that was at risk, I had to go through with it. But she was becoming a major distraction for me in a good way. Tori embodied all I wanted in a woman minus the perfect figure. I know I am wrong for agreeing to help Eureka destroy her, but I have always been in love with Eureka and saying no to her was like being a crack addicted trying to kick the habit cold turkey.

After leaving Eureka another voice message and a few short texts, I started thinking back on days when I came into the fashion industry, I'd gotten an internship at Gucci, and it taught me many things good and bad, and some were downright ugly.

There is where I learned how to master manipulation. Selling a dream to someone who is

137

hungry, is like getting away with murder. Their desire, desperation, and drive will overshadow their rational thinking and Tori is right for the picking her loneliness and hint of desperation along with hurt makes her very weak.

Channel surfing to occupy my time until Eureka hit me back, I came across an ad for a pair of jeans, jeans that I designed when I was nineteen for the internship program at Gucci.

These jeans were supposed to change the industry for men and women. I designed them specifically for a tight fit around the legs and accentuate the area around the bottom.

"Fuckin thief, this was mine." I said frustratingly as the name Raulph Lauren and his new fall collection's commercial was on the screen.

"Those are mine, fuckin snake. Winstel, you will pay. I designed those jeans."

One night all of us were at a celebration party at one of the top executives at the company's mansion for the new summer lineup for Gucci that was set to be released later that week.

I had a few too many so I found a room to sober up before the long drive back to my loft in the city. I closed my eyes for what seemed like a minute, but I felt something wet and warm on my dick, when I opened my eyes all I could see was the top of someone's head bobbing up and down.

The more whoever it went down on my dick the wetter their mouth got. I tried to focus my eyes, but the liquor had my head spinning and eyes crossed so I relaxed my body and allowed whomever it was to work me into an eruption.

"You like that baby?" a deep voice spoke.

My eye widen and I was able to focus a little more. There standing in front of me wiping his lips off my load was the executive, my boss's son. Then I turned my head and could see my so-called best friend holding his cell phone in a corner.

He held his camera phone laughing as he recorded the whole incident.

The Executive's son wasn't amused and looked shocked and confused. "Didn't you ask for me Hen?" he said as he looked over at me with big doe eyes.

140

"No, I fuckin didn't. I don't get down like that. I love pussy."

Winstel, my ex-best friend laughed and laughed until I jumped up and knocked the executive's son to the floor. I lounged at Winstel ready to lay him out and take his phone. Holding the phone in front of him he said, "Lay one hand on me, and I will make sure everyone in the company including his father gets this video in a matter of seconds." He turned his cellphone towards me to show me the video. He'd already had it ready to share on every social media site and company e-mail registry in our circle.

The fact that the son was in the closet and his father valued the public's opinion of his career it

141

would ruin us both. He would disown his son then black ball me so I would never work in the industry again.

 I put my hand down and walked out leaving. The design was still with my ex-best friend, because I used his laptop, took all the credit and claimed the design as his own.

That night life taught me a hell of a lesson. Trust no one.

 I turned the TV off. Walking over to the mini bar in my room I picked up my cellphone trying to contact Eureka one more time.

She still didn't pick up so I texted her. 'Baby girl, call me when you get this. I have made so much progress with this Tori chic, she won't know what hit her.'

After leaving her that message, I felt some type of way. Tori was a good woman and pretty at that and she defiantly didn't deserve what Eureka and I were about to serve her, but I will do anything for love even if I have to pay the price.

Chapter 16

Love has a hold of me

I sat at the foot of Eureka's bed for days. Praying once again for a miracle. Life for her has been one let down after another and I know she was hurting because of the loss of our son, but I had no idea she'd turned to drugs. When my car flipped over, I suffered a broken arm and a few cuts to my face. But Eureka... Eureka suffered the most. She was thrown out of the car, all because she wasn't in a seat belt. She suffered two broken ribs and her left leg was shattered along with a huge scar across her face. The doctors felt it would be best to put her in a medically induced coma.

I tried to tell myself how I would break the news to her about her scare and her condition. The doctors told me that Eureka was pregnant about 12 weeks along, I knew it wasn't mine because I hadn't touched her in months. But somehow I still feel like this is my fault. My love for Tori and all I missed and wanted in her on almost daily was the reason I felt Eureka started acting the way she did. Now she is laid up in the bed clinging on for dear life.

"Mr. Collinsworth, can I get you anything?" A young nurse came in the room with medications to put into Eureka's IV bag.

"No I'm okay, by the way, thank you for taking such good care of my wife."

"No thanks needed, it's my job to make sure all of the patients are comfortable and the families as well. You have to heal the spirit first then the body will follow." She said with a smile.

It struck me odd because that is a phrase my mother use to say when I would watch her work at her medical practice.

"What is your name? I would like to send you something, although you say it's your job, but I really appreciate you."

"Well if you insist, my name is Renita Tomas."

"Well, nurse Tomas, thank you again and I will have something to you shortly."

She and I smiled as She continued to administer the medication into the IV bag after she was done she cleaned up then turned to leave the room.

She got to the door, "oh before I forget, I have your wife's belongings. The officers dropped them off last week and I put them up, some of the night shift

146

nurses moved them to the lost and found. When I asked them had they seen the bag, they told me where it was so I went and got it back. I will be back in a second to give them to you."

I thanked her, then laid my head on top of Eureka's hand. I felt so much hurt.

This once vibrant sexy, gorgeous woman was killing herself because of me. How could I live with myself if she dies or her baby? I made a vow at that moment that when and if she pulls through this I will devote my time and life to her and her baby. I will raise the child as my own. I was so consumed with guilt that anything I would do to save her even if that means losing my life to do it.

Nurse Tomas came back in the room with a clear bag filled with Eureka's belongings. Her purse and

147

dress she wore that night was there. I wanted to let her sisters know about her condition so I opened the bag to see if her cell phone was inside. I didn't see it so I opened her purse.

Rambling through the papers and small pieces of lace material inside of the purse, I came across a small pill bottom filled with small white football shaped pills. I put the bottle down and shook my head. Feeling even guiltier, I realized the pills were drugs. I found her cell phone and powered it on.

Almost immediately the notifications caused the phone to vibrate back to back. There were quite a few missed calls with the England, London area code, then I noticed a couple text messages. I tried to check them, but there was lock code. I took one attempt and it didn't unlock the screen, then I thought about Eureka's favorite number, the same

148

number she uses for almost everything. "7713" I spoke as I keyed it in.

The phone unlocked and I went to the text messages. The first few were from different modeling gigs across the city. I almost dropped the phone when I noticed a few conversations she held with her supplier. The sad part was I knew this snake, I called him a good friend at one time in our lives, but I guess money is the motivation to all things good or evil.

I searched and searched lookin for more messages from Royal and how much he was charging her for heroin. Holding the phone downward, I almost through it across the room. Out of frustration, I continued to go through a few more messages. I stopped at one from someone named Hen.

149

Hen: Hey love, glad to see made it home safe. I will be sure to call you as soon as the plan is a go. Love You'.

Eureka: Thank you, it was a pleasure seeing you again. And the sex was amazing. Make sure you get to her good and in love. Her fat ass will pay.

I scrolled through about 200 hundred or more messages between the two of them. The last few were days before the accident. I couldn't take seeing all of the deceptions she'd had going on and now she is laying her fighting for her life. I put the phone back in her purse.

Getting up from the chair about to walk in front of the window to clear my mind and gather my thoughts, I heard her phone vibrating inside of her purse. I stopped for a moment contemplating whether I should answer it. As soon as I took a step to pick up the phone it stopped.

I heard the sound of a notification so I picked it back up to see. And it was a text message from the Hen person. I read the message with disbelief when he mentioned Tori's name. I wanted to shake Eureka awake to see what she and her friend were talking about Tori. I pressed the little phone receiver icon at the top of the message, I was about to find out who Hen was and how does he know about Tori.

I held up the phone to my ear and about on the third ring a deep voice answered,

"Bae, where have you been? I've been worried sick about you." He Conerly asked.

"Well this is not bae, in fact, this is bae's husband. How in the fuck do you know my wife?"

A moment of silence invaded the moment as I awaited his response. Feeling ready to go all the way off, I open my mouth to ask again but was cut off with laughter.

"Oh, so this is the pretty boy JC, the one who has my Eureka so messed up in the head. Let me ask you then where is she? I have been trying to reach her for days. What the fuck have you done to her?"

Showing me no respect he asked me as if I was the side piece or boyfriend.

"She good muthafucka. She laid up right where she need to be. Now whats this situation you got going on? And what does it have to do with Tori?" Mentioning Tori's name caused me to become more frustrated and desperate to know just what they had going on and why she was even in his cipher.

"Aww, sweet voluptuous Tori, she is easy on the eyes. Her hips round and that pussy hood, as she and her friend Val is it likes to call it let's just say I have fun playing mechanic underneath it."

He started laughing. The way her name rolled off his tongue and his description of her confirmed what I feared, he'd, in fact, was talking about Tori.

Seething with anger I gripped her cellphone as if I was choking the life out of this Hen. I normally conducted myself in a manner full of professionalism, but at this moment all of my street came rushing out of me like a hail of bullets flying everywhere, "look Hen, homie or whatever the fuck your name is. What the fuck you and my slutbag of a wife got going on besides you and her

153

fuckin? And what in the fuck does that have to do with Tori?"

"Look dawg, tell Eureka to give me a ring ole chap, when she can. We got some finishing touches to put on this masterpiece. Oh and if you treated your woman right, then there would know me." He sinisterly laughed as he hung up the phone in my face. I immediately tried dialing the number back, but each time went to voicemail. I looked through their messages one more time and just like I suspected there were some photos of him and his dick and just like my wife loves to show off there were a few pussy and body shoots of her. Now that I know what he looks like I will be sure to find out everything about him.

I looked over at an unconscious Eureka wanting to choke whats left of her life right up out of her.

154

I walked out of her room down to the elevator. If I'd stayed a second longer, I would have been locked up for murder. I got on the elevator and pressed the ground floor button. My new car was parked in the space located right under the wing of the hospital where Eureka's room was located. I was spending all my days and nights up there by her bedside, stressing and worrying will she make it and now … well, I don't care about what happens to her at this moment. I need to get to Tori and warn her about whatever this thing is Eureka and this Hen has set up for her.

Chapter 17

Beneficial union

"Girl you better be hitting that. I mean come on Tori how long you gonna keep ya kitty locked down. JC has moved on now it's time you do the same sis. Are you too big and sexy wit it to be in hibernation like this. 2 years? Fa'real 2 long ass years? Shiddd. Ah, bitch like I would have bust it opens the first day that fine ass Hennry said hello."

Val and I laughed hard. She had a point tho. Hennry was for some odd reason turning the charm up several notches and I had to admit it was getting to me. For the past week, we have spent serval nights working on this new launch. His Dakar for men cologne was an inviting and intoxicating scent. He would lean close to me pretending to look over some sketches. But I could feel his breath on my neck making me moist.

"Girl you right. I don't know how much longer I can resist him. I might have to get me a piece of that chocolate."

"Yass...sass, now that's my hot bitch. How is my pretty niece? Did she like her bike?"

"Oh my god she won't stay off of it. I swear if I would let her sleep with it on her bed she would. But she is growing like a weed. I think she takes her height from her daddy. Speaking of how is he and his wife doing."

"Girl hell if I know. I haven't heard from him in a while. He used to call and on the low ask about you, but I haven't heard from him in about a month or more. Anyway, forget about him."

"How can I Val? I have a lifetime reminder. Every time I look at her, I see him. Some days I wished I would have told him I was pregnant. But I didn't want that evil Heffa and me into it fighting for his love. I know her, she would have tried to use their son as leverage and I wasn't about to go through that. Okay, enough about him let me go so I can get ready for this meeting with Hennry."

"Okay Love you, sis. I will see you soon. I will be there in about two weeks. Oh, see if Hennry has a friend."

I laughed but knew how serious Val was. "Okay, I got you, oh he does have a younger finer brother maybe we can hit the town together.

"Okay kiss my niece." We said our goodbyes then I got up to make sure Samya was okay with the sitter.

I called Hennry to let him know I would be a little late. Samya was a little fussy. Once I calmed her down and made sure she was in bed sound asleep, I took my shower and got dressed.

Feeling a little nervous, I primped myself in the mirror. I sprayed some Juicy contour perfume on the right spots.

"Ok, now you look flawless," I spoke to my reflection.

I grabbed my purse and walked in Samya's room kissed her on the forehead then walked outside to my car.

"I 'm not scared of lions, tigers, and bears. But I'm scared of-" The lyrics of Jasmine Sullivan's single came on the radio as soon as I started up my car.

159

I shifted the gear into drive and pulled off. The ride was full of wonder and fantasy for me. I wondered would Hennry want to go the next level or will we continue to play this game of chase.

Pulling up to the office I spotted Hennry's car parked on the side of the building. I got out of my car and walked over to his. There was a note on the windshield.

'Hey, there sexy lady I felt we could use a night out. Meet me at Shalou's Bistro. Park your car, I

160

have arranged for a car service to pick you up. See you soon'

Hennry

I smiled and placed the note in my purse. I looked over at a pair of flashing headlights attached to a black limo. I walked over as the driver step out and opened the back door for me to have a seat. I sat down in the plush seats and sip on a glass of champagne to ease my nerves. I wondered what Hennry had in store for me.

******

Pulling up to the Bistro, I noticed rose petals trailing from the curb to the front door. The driver parked and got out to open my door before one of my feet could touch the concrete two attendants stood on either side pulling a roll of red fabric.

Amazed and shocked I stepped out of the limo feeling like a celebrity walking the red carpet. I made it to the front door as one of the attendants opened it for me to walk inside, I spotted Hennry standing at a table looking fine as ever. He wore a red and black button up and a pair of black fitted Polo jeans. His wrist was iced with a Marc Jacob watch with a matching chain.

"Have a seat my dear. You look scrumptious."

After he made sure that I was sitting in my seat, he then sat down in his.

162

Looking around noticed there were only a few other people sitting at their tables.

"Would you like anything to eat or drink?" Hennry asked with a slight smirk.

"Yes, I will have a glass of wine and a salad."

"Of course, and I will have the waiter bring your salad right over to st- I mean bring it over."

His comment, or quickness to clean it caught me off guard because he was usually so compassionate. Sometimes He would even suggest that I have a low carb meal or drink because I was really working on losing some weight. I shook it off and started small talk with him. He seemed a little distracted but still flattering as usual.

We sipped on some champagne until we were both were more than a little intoxicated. Hennry

163

decided that we should go to a rooftop party being held by one of his friends at a nearby hotel. It was still early so I agreed.

When we getting out of the Limousine. Hennry lost his footing just a little. But he quickly got his balance and we proceeded to walk into the lobby of a very luxurious and swanky hotel. Hennry told the driver he could come up and chill or he can take the limo and be back in a couple of hours.

The driver said he would call Hennry's cell phone to see when we'd be ready to leave.

When got on the elevator Hennry stood in front of me and placed a soft kiss on my lips, "Tori you are, baby, you are a beautiful woman. I hope tonight is as memorable for you as it will be for me."

Feeling some of the bubbly from earlier, "I know it will be." The elevators doors chimed opened. The scene was one that I was very familiar with.

All of the females in attendance were small, skinny and models. A few of them I'd seen on various commercials. Hennry held my hand as we made our way through the party.

He introduced me to a few other designers and models. I ended up passing out some business cards, then we found a seat In the back and sat down.

A gentleman walked over and spoke. He was real polite, but I got the feeling that Hennry didn't care for him.

With one side of his lips curled, he looked as if he strained to return the hello. The gentleman extended his hand to me, I stretched mine out to be polite and he kissed the back of my hand.

"Okay, have a lovely day ole chap."

Hennry forced a smirk, "you to ole…chap."

Looking at the both of them no matter how pleasant they sounded anyone who was standing there would notice there was some beef between the two of them.

Once the gentlemen walk off Hennry mumbled something under his breath.

"Are you okay? Who was that? You seemed to really dislike him."

"I'm fine sexy lady, he was an old business associate, but I'm okay. Let's enjoy this night."

166

He raised his arm to signal for a server to come over. He orders another bottle of champagne and for me a long Island iced tea.

I sipped on the drink for the remainder of the night. I knew I had to get home to Samya. Hennry, on the other hand, was drunk. I mean out of his mind drunk.

"Okay, okay it's time we get out of here I have to get home to my little girl. I stood up but was quickly pulled back down rather roughly by Hennry.

"No... I'm sorry sexy. I didn't mean to pull you like that. Seems this liquor has me feeling my courage." He said with slurred speech.

"I'm fine, but we have to get home. I have a baby and you have to finish your layout."

167

"I'm sorry Tori, I had something planned for us tonight and I blew it. I shouldn't have allowed that clown make me so upset. I tell you what, I have a room downstairs. Sorry if I was presumptuous, but I really wanted to take our relationship to another level. Can we still use the room? Not to make love or anything like that, but to sleep this off so it won't go to waste."

 The hour was late and the long island iced tea drink I had done have my head spinning a little. I thought for a moment then agreed to stay. I called the sitter to check on Samya and see if she would stay with her for the night.

"How's the lil tike and will the nanny be able to stay? Hennry asked slumped over in his chair. He was digging sluggishly in his jacket pocket and pulled out a card. He passed it to me. It was a keycard for room 671.

168

I helped him stand to his feet and walked over toward the elevator.

The same gentlemen from earlier walked over and offered to help, "see some things never change. Still can't handle a few drinks um Hen." I detected a hint of sarcasm and declined his help. Hennry, on the other hand, was ready to swing. It took all I had to hold him back. The gentlemen laughed and laughed as if he was taunting Hennry.

The gentlemen shouted something I couldn't make out because the music was so loud, but judging Hennry's reaction he heard it well. Sobering up almost instantly, Hennry grabbed my arm and we got on the elevator.

He was ranting the whole ride to the 6th floor. I didn't know what to say or even ask. About the guy. We got to the room and opened the door.

169

Stepping inside, there were candles and as an assortment of different colored rose petals everywhere. Hennry walked over to the plush sofa in the forge and sat down. I joined him. Rubbing my hand gently on his shoulders, he opened up to me,

"I'm am so sorry Tori. I really wanted this to be a special night. The guy downstairs was someone I held close to my heart, we were like brothers until he betrayed me. When I first came into the fashion world, he and I held some of the same dreams and aspirations, and that was to make it big. We started interning at the Raulph Lauren office under some of the top designers. Well, I came up with a revolutionary design for some jeans. You may have heard of them, they are all the rave here, anyway he set me up to be a very embarrassing and compromising position which could have ended my career. I would have been blackballed throughout

170

the industry. So I choose to leave the internship, but he held my designs in his computer and I never had the design patented, so he claimed them as his own."

"Hennry you are very talented. You will be a success, especially with this new launch. He won't know what hit him. As for the jeans, you can come up with some better and market them to plus size women. We are always looking for the right jeans to flatten our stomachs and raise up our butts. I know all too well about betrayal and hurt, but you don't allow it to take you out of your true self. Always shine and do good and good will follow, no good deed goes unrewarded."

Hennry turned and looked me in my eyes and kissed me. I pulled away, not wanting to confuse drunk sex with anything meaningful.

171

"Tori, I know we haven't known each other for a long time but I have to say tonight and the past few days, you have shown me that you are everything I have been searching for. Can I be completely honest with you?"

Feeling some concern because I didn't know what he was about to tell me I reluctantly shook my head yes.

"Tori please what I'm about to say, please don't take it the wrong way. But I want to be honest with you. Begin is the fashion industry, you are exposed to so many things all colors and shapes, but I was always accustom to smaller women. Not because they were better as far as looks, but that is the world we created here and ... and that's the only world I knew. Tori, I want to explore something deeper with you, I mean really meaningful if you will allow me. No this is not the liquor talking but me, Hennry."

Taking every word he spoke into my heart and mind, I paused a moment. I have had men in my life to confess but not like this. Down to the core, the average big girl might take it a sign to get up and out of there but to me at least he came real and told me.

"I respect that Hennry, some men won't even come clean like that. I must say tho you really didn't come off like that to me. I mean your eye and detail to design for a plus sized woman is remarkable to say the least, but you have swept me off my feet on many occasions. I am feeling you as well and I would also like to see where we can take this."

This time, I leaned forward and kissed his full, soft lips.

173

He caressed my hands and our tongues danced inside of each other's mouths. I could feel his body relaxing as we began to caressing and touching each other.

Fondling my erect nipples through my shirt, I could feel the warmth of his breath against the nape of my neck.

Just as I was about to remove his shirt, my cell phone vibrated." Excuse me a second this might be about my baby." I looked at the screen and noticed Val was calling. I quickly pushed the end button and sent her a quick text.

Me: look, missy, I'm taking your advice and about to get me a taste of chocolate I'll hit you up in the am. Love you, sis.

I turned my phone completely off, "now where were we?"

174

He smiled devilishly, "we were right about her." He lowered his body in front of me and started pulling my panties down from under my skirt.

"You want to take a shower first?" I asked in a low lustful tone as he worked my center with his index finger.

"No need for that." He slipped his finger out of my honey put and put into his lips and lip and licked my nectar from them. "I want to taste the natural you."

With my dress pushed up to my mid-section, he took one of my legs and placed it on one side of the couch and the other one on the opposite side, exposing my clean perfectly shaven twat.

I tried to take my heels off so that I could get more comfortable, "no, leave them on. Tori I want to

175

remove your clothes myself. Every article you are wearing I want to remove them with my teeth."

Lowering his head, he began feasting on my clit. He nobbled on my thighs and kissed them with gentleness and ease. Taking his tongue, he stroked a trail down to my ankles. Removing one of my heels, he placed my toes in his mouth. He licked and sucked on each of them, making sure he gave them special attention. He repeated the same move on my other foot.

 He came back up to my wet now juicy center and pulled at the crease of the lips, he placed his tongue right on the spot. Looking down at him our eyes met. It was like an unspoken sign for him to feat more.

He suddenly grabbed my thighs and held them open eagle with a gentle force as he licked and slurped like an animal. Growling and slurping sounds filled the room.

Starting to feel my body tense, I tried to push his head back to give me some relief, but to no avail he continued to work me into a sexual explosion I hadn't felt in years.

"Yes...yes...yes!" moan of bliss echoed through the room.

I tried catching my breath as Henry hurried and undressed before I could move.

My legs fell out of tired as I tried to sit up to join him.

I was about to pull my dress over my head, "no, baby I'm not down with you." He quickly laid me back, then lowered himself to his knees as my bottom half hung off the couch.

177

In a sudden move of passion he kissed my inner thighs then went directly back to my wet clit. He kissed, tugged and caressed my clit with his tongue; I was sex drunk. He was taking my composure away and I loved it. I started pinching my own nipples, I placed my hand down in the middle of my thighs to open my pussy lips wider, exposing my clit more as if I was feeding him.

"Yes, that's it, show me that pink. I love this. I never knew what I've been missing."

 His lust filled moans mixed with words of desire had me feeling like the best was yet to come.

He licked and sucked my center for hours giving me multiple orgasms.

Finally, he eased up enough to remove my dress and carry me to the bed.

178

Positioning my back against the pillow, I watched as he lowered his body on top of mine. He reaching his hand behind my back he un-snap my bra.

My size 44dd breast spilled out, he quickly place both nipples inside of his mouth ravishing each of them. We were lost in each other for the rest of the night.

He'd kissed me in places that had been neglected since JC. What grabbed me more was the fact that he was like a kid in a new toy store, reaching, grabbing and kissing everything that was new to him for the first time.

******

Laying in his arms I struggled to open my eyes as the sunlight crept through the blinds of the window. Hennry was sound asleep with a smile across his lips.

I took a deep breath. Remembering the moments of passion, we shared last night. I needed that release and was very pleased it was with him.

"Mmm, good morning beautiful," Hennry said smiling from ear to ear. I cuddle underneath his arm ready for another round until I noticed the time on the clock beside the bed on the nightstand.

"Oh shit! I have to get home." I jumped up and put my clothes on.

I grabbed my purse and phone from the night stand, gave Hennry a kiss and rushed out of the door. When I got to my car I turned my cellphone on to call the sitter and let her know I was on my way home.

When the phone powered on full, I had over ten missed calls and five text messages from Val.

I dialed her number and she answered on the first ring, "what is wrong? Girl somebody better been done died the way you called me all night."

"Please tell me, sis, you didn't sleep with Hennry last night."

"Yes, I sure did. I took your advice and gave in and it was good too. Why? You told me to get me some. What's with the change of heart?"

Val was silent. I came to a stop light, "Val, hello."

"Sis I'm sorry, but there is something you should know. I got a call from JC last night and, and...."

"Come on Val say it."

"I don't know how to say this, but Hennry knows Eureka a-"

Just as she was about to tell me the call dropped. I tried to drive as fast as I could to get home. I was going to call her when I get home because I was sure I heard wrong.

Chapter 18

Can't run from destiny

Thoughts rambled through JC's mind as he tried to figure out what exactly was going on. He always wondered why Tori just up and moved instead of staying to fight for what they had. He started replaying scenes in his mind about the encounters they'd had and how awkward he felt when he would see her after he left Miami. So many times he wanted to call her, to make things right but something or someone would always seem to get in the way.

"Man so what are yo gonna do?" Quentin asked as they sat at the bar drinking on some Hennessey

V.S.O.P. JC was so deep into thoughts he hadn't heard his phone ringing.

"JC, man yo phone been ringing off the off. You gon answer it?"

He looked down at the phone and noticed it was the hospital, and he sent it straight to his voicemail. The fact he was furious with Eureka had him not concerned about her or what condition she was in.

"Man Scoop, I have seen some pretty low down stunts pulled throughout my life, but Eureka takes the cake. All this time I have been feeling guilty and turning myself inside out to help her, but this…. This poor excuse of a woman was playing games the whole time. Now I need to see what she has done to Tori with this Hen person."

185

JC seethed with anger as he thought on the 'what ifs'. He was all too familiar with the whys, but the, 'what ifs' were what had him on edge.

"Hey you know Eureka and females like her always want to be on top. Thy hate losing but I don't think she is that crazy to hurt Tori. Why don't you call Val and see if Tori's okay." Joshua tried to reason with JC when he noticed JC clutching his glass tightly in his hand until it started to crack.

"You right, you right. Let me check this voicemail right fast th- no I'ma call Val now."

JC dialed Val's number and waited with more and more thoughts ransacking his mind, until she picked up.

"hello." She said sounding groggy.

"I'm sorry Val, did I wake you?"

186

"Yes. And who is this?"

"Im sorry, this me JC. I needed to talk to you about Tori."

"JC do you know what time it is? Hell my hair still sleep. Can't what you need to talk to me about Tori wait until the respectable time in the morning? No offense bru but this bitch needs her beauty sleep."

Val wasn't pleasant when she is awakened in the wee hours of the morning, but JC was desperate to see if Tori was okay. He began telling Val all the things he found out concerning Hen and Eureka. By the time he was done Val was wide awake and alert, ready to call Tori and warn her.

JC wondered what Val was talking about when she said she needed to call Tori and make sure 'they are okay.' JC told Val to call him when she gets in touch with Tori. He didn't want to cal her himself

187

out fear and more but he knew if one person that could get to Tori it would be Val.

Chapter 19

So you think is all good?

Thoughts rambled through JC's mind as he tried to figure out what exactly was going on. He always wondered why Tori just up and moved instead of staying to fight for what they had. He started replaying scenes in his mind about the encounters they'd had and how awkward he felt when he would see her after he left Miami. So many times he wanted to call her, to make things right, but something or someone would always seem to get in the way.

"Man so what are yo gonna do?" Quentin asked as they sat at the bar drinking on some Hennessey V.S.O.P. JC was so deep into thoughts he hadn't heard his phone ringing.

"JC, man yo phone been ringing off the off. You gon answer it?"

He looked down at the phone and noticed it was the hospital, and he sent it straight to his voicemail. The fact he was furious with Eureka had him not concerned about her or what condition she was in.

"Man Scoop, I have seen some pretty low down stunts pulled throughout my life, but Eureka takes the cake. All this time I have been feeling guilty and turning myself inside out to help her, but this…. This poor excuse of a woman was playing games the whole time. Now I need to see what she has done to Tori with this Hen person."

190

JC seethed with anger as he thought on the 'what ifs'. He was all too familiar with the whys, but the, 'what ifs' were what had him on edge.

"Hey you know Eureka and females like her always want to be on top. Thy hate losing, but I don't think she is that crazy to hurt Tori. Why don't you call Val and see if Tori's okay." Joshua tried to reason with JC when he noticed JC clutching his glass tightly in his hand until it started to crack.

"You right, you right. Let me check this voicemail right fast th- no I'ma call Val now."

JC dialed Val's number and waited with more and more thoughts ransacking his mind until she picked up.

"Hello," She said sounding groggy.

"I'm sorry Val, did I wake you?"

191

"Yes. And who is this?"

"I'm sorry, this me JC. I needed to talk to you about Tori."

"JC do you know what time it is? Hell, my hair still sleep. Can't what you need to talk to me about Tori wait until the respectable time in the morning? No offense bro but this bitch needs her beauty sleep."

Val wasn't pleasant when she is awakened in the wee hours of the morning, but JC was desperate to see if Tori was okay. He began telling Val all the things he found out concerning Hen and Eureka. By the time, he was done Val was wide awake and alert, ready to call Tori and warn her.

JC wondered what Val was talking about when she said she needed to call Tori and make sure 'they are okay.' JC told Val to call him when she gets in touch with Tori. He didn't want to claim her himself

192

out fear and more, but he knew if one person that could get to Tori it would be Val.

So you think is all good?

"Mrs. Collinsworth, you are doing so much better. We have tried calling your husband for you several times, but no answers but don't worry, we will leave him another message." A nice nurse came into my room several times checking to make sure I was okay and gave me medication. I looked at my phone and noticed Hennry called and left several voice messages. I started worrying if JC had seen any of them.

Feeling the huge bandage wrapped on the sides of my face, I couldn't help but wonder what was underneath. Coming back from the dead, literally, had me feeling some type of way.

Feeling of remorse sadness and more came rushing through the tears that were streaming now my cheeks. I felt like my life was over and my career, I was uncertain.

I tried to calling JC one more time myself, but I couldn't see the numbers clearly out of my right eye because of the bandage, so I decided to put my phone up.

When I placed it on the side of the bed it started vibrating.

194

I picked it up and answered it, "hello."

"Hello love, how have you been? I have been trying to call you for weeks."

I smiled hearing the concern in his voice. Although it wasn't my husband, this one the one person who has never let me down, no matter what.

"Hennry... I am so happy to hear your voice. How are you?"

"I'm good love, what about you? I have been calling and sending messages to your phone for days. I tried to tell you what happened, but pretty boy answered your phone. Eureka he knows about us."

I began to put the pieces together, JC hadn't been up at the hospital since I woke up from the coma and now he wasn't even answering his phone. Now I know why.

195

"Hennry how and why on earth did you tell him about us? Did you make any moves on Tori we are going to have to wrap this up soon?"

"I don't know how and what he knows about us, but he knows nothing about what I'm trying to do to Tori but judging his tone he will find out. Eureka there is something else I need to tell you."

Hennry's tone became somber and low, "Baby girl...I-"

"Come on spit it out. Hennry. I have to do some damage control."

His silence was deafing. "Eureka I can't go through with this. I really have some feeling for Tori. I mean she really is a great woman and an even better mother. I really want to see this go to another level with her. I'm sorry."

"I KNEW IT! All you men are fuckin weak. I have been in the hospital fighting for my life and this one thing I asked you to do, you failed. What is wrong with you men and what does hold does this big fat bitch have on you all? It's okay you can skip off into the sunset with her fat ass, but you, JC or that damn bastard child will live to see a moment of bliss."

"Eureka! Eureka! What is wrong with you? You are so miserable that you are willing to hurt an innocent child over it?"

I started to laugh, when I thought about the pain I was about to put on all of them who I felt wronged me. ALL YOU MUTHAFUCKAS GON PAY!"

197

Eureka, this is not worth it. Heal yourself and make something of your life. You still have your career just let this go."

When he mentioned my career had me to pause and think of this bandage on my face. "Hold on." I said getting up from the bed and hobbled over to my medical chart.

I started reading all the diagnosis and treatments.

"What a fuck! Scar, right cheek, skin graph! Oh my god 12weeks." I was livid and scared at the same time after reading about all of the surgeries, medications and the many reconstructive procedures I have gone through since the accident on my chart.

I heard Hennry yelling through the phone. I hobbled back over to it and hung it up. I pressed the nurse call button, I wanted out of there and now. I would make sure Tori pays dearly for taking everything that was mine.

Chapter 20

You can't stop whats meant to be

Are you okay? How's my niece? Please tell me you didn't sleep with him, did you?"

"Slow down sis, what's with all of the questions. I'm fine and Samya is fine. What the matter?"

Sounding nervous Val shoots question after question.

"Calm down now tell me what's going on. Valerie, you are scaring me."

"I'm sorry sis, I was worried after I have tried to call you all last night. Listen Hennry knows Eureka."

"Are you sure? I don't understand, Hennry knows Eureka? Where did you hear this and why is it important? I knew sooner or later I would run into some people she would know, after all she is a model." I chuckled.

"Sis this is not funny, I think the man has been playing you. JC called me last night. He and Eureka were in a car accident and he found out about Hennry through text messages between he and Eureka and your name was mentioned. "Val was stuttering and crying.

"Val maybe she was telling him about me for business purposes. Come on sis calm down."

"Tori, it didn't sound like it was as innocent as that. JC was really worried, hell he called me in the wee

200

hours in the morning and you know how I am when somebody wakes me up from my beauty sleep. Once he got my full attention, sis I swear I could hear how worried he was, he got me all nervous. He made me promise to call you before I got off the phone with him."

I noticed a call coming in on the other line. I pulled the phone down from my ear and noticed it was Hennry. I let the voicemail pick it up. I wanted to see what else JC told Val.

"Val I will talk to Hennry and see where his head is. He has been nothing but nice to me and last night, well let's just say it was more than I could have ever imagined. He was really into me, I and mean all of me. He even told me I was the first BBW he'd ever been with."

I smiled thinking of the warm and soft and very attentive kisses Hennry placed all over my body last night, from head to toe.

"Okay sis but make sure you be careful. I hope he hasn't told Eureka about Samya I don't want nothing happening to my niece."

"I will, and make sure you get those models out here as soon as possible Hennry's new lineup will take the industry by storm."

I promised to call her and to be careful with Hennry. I knew when it comes to a woman scorned like Eureka nothing is impossible. I think I will give her a call to let her know woman to woman she won, she got what and who she wanted.

I picked Samya up and kissed her. Checking her forehead to make sure she didn't still have a slight fever. She felt better and her baby chatter was

202

music to my ears. Looking her, rubbing my finger through her thick curly hair made me wish for innocent days but I wouldn't trade her for anything in the world.

I wondered if I should tell JC about her. ?as I robbing her of a father? And did JC have a right to know? Or should I just stay here in my own little world. Looked right into her innocent face, "you want to know your father Sue- sue? She smiled and said something in her baby chatter then continued to play with her toy. I knew she would be able to answer me, but I wanted a sign to tell him or not.

I played with her a few seconds more then set her down inside of her playpen, "mommy will be right back. I have to make a hard phone call." I kissed her cheek and walked into the other room. If Eureka was still as feisty and she was the last time I saw her, this conversation wouldn't be pretty.

203

Chapter 21

Woman to Woman

Taking a deep breath I dialed Eureka's number. On the third ring it went to voicemail. I took a sigh of relief not really wanting get into it with her. I knew she somehow knew about my daughter or Hennry may have innocently told her, but I have to smooth this all out and fast before JC finds out. I will tell him but on my terms.

 My phone rang as I was putting it on the table. Picking it back up, I looked at the screen. I took and deep breath and mustered up some politeness, "Hello Eureka, how are you?"

"Who is this?" Eureka said with a hint of agitation.

"This is Tori. How are you?"

"Um, im just fine. Why are you calling me?"

"I heard about the accident and wanted to see if you were okay. I also heard we have a mutual acquaintance, Hennry?"

I heard her clear her throat, "Oh im fine, so you can put your big girl panties back in your drawer. I'm not dead so you won't be getting my husband. Tori listen fat bitch I don't want or need your calls of concern for me or shall I say for my husband. I am his wife not you. So I suggest you move on."

Taking a moment not to react to her nastiness, I thought of the words I was going to say.

"Look Eureka, you don't like me and I get that but how do you know Hennry? And why does JC think im in danger?"

"Oh so you have been talking to my husband? You fat home wrecking bitch. I swear when I get my hands on you and that ugly ass little girl... Im going to make you wish you never knew a J or a C."

Hearing her say something about my daughter confirmed she knew about her. I wasn't going to tolerate her disrespecting my child,

"look here you simple minded little twit, I know you have had some rough stuff going on and yea now I know that you know about my child , but what you will not do is disrespect her in any way. Your problem is with me so ya need to mind your mouth."

"Hahaha, really you fat disgusting bitch? I swear you have become a real problem. First my son dies because of you. Then you have my husband's child... and the one person that has always been by my side has left me hanging because of you. Oh no

206

Tori you need to mind your mouth and your business."

"You know what Eureka, I have tried to be nice to you but here is what it really is… you are the cause for all of your problems not me. I am sorry for one thing, the death of JC's son. That was something I wouldn't wish on my worst enemy, but maybe that was a good thing for the baby, I mean look at you, you are a horrible person and full of bull shit. The old saying beauty is only skin deep but ugly is down to the soul is so true because you are all of that. Maybe you should try to focus on your mental health other than a man."

I knew what I said would push her to a point but she'd pushed me too far. The one thing no one will do his hurt me or my baby, not JC and most defiantly not her.

She didn't respond. Over flowing with anger I was about to hang the phone up in her face. But she said something that caused me to stop cold.

"A' Tori, Tick- tock, tick- tock, tick –tock, let's see if you can see the time on the clock."

Out of nowhere, started a rhyme that was eerie and odd. It didn't have anything to do with the moment.

"Listen you crazy ass Heffa, if you come anywhere near me or my baby I w-"

"YOU WILL WHAT! WHAT! Do shit. You won't see me coming. Just like you didn't see Hennry. I knew that was all it would take to get your fat ass right where I knew you to be heart broken and useless all because my husband choose me. Sad how you really thought crossing me was going to somehow be okay. Oh by the way, how do you think JC will handle finding out about this little ugly ass love child of yours. See pretty always wins."

Panicking I yelled her name, but she'd hung up. I knew I needed to tell JC before she does and somehow keep my baby safe. There is no way in hell she will ever be around this nut job.

Chapter 22

Things in the dark do find light

For what seemed like the 9 thousandth time my phone rang and each time I sent it right to voice mail. Val called me back after she talked to Tori to let me know she was okay.

I started to replay the night of the accident right before the crash Eureka said something about Tori and a baby, I thought she was just high out of her mind until when I called Val the other night and she said she will call and check on them. "Them? Who is them?" I said aloud as I began rubbing my temples.

Lately, my head has been pounding. Eureka called daily and the hospital aw well, to let me know she was out of her coma and that she'd took her bandages off. Just like I knew it would go, she didn't take the sight of herself to well. The staff told me that she was throwing things and even fought a few nurses.

Thinking of all the drama Eureka has caused me in my life had my mind all over the place. But one thing was for sure, I still was concerned about Tori.

I picked up the large envelope from the table that my lawyer sent.

Pulling out the huge stack of papers inside, I thought about the decision I'd made to divorce Eureka was the right one. It was the time that I was   honest with myself and her. Tori remains on my heart and mind daily.

Feeling the vibration from my cell phone, I looked at it once again and sent the caller to the voicemail.

"I really don't have time for this bullshit," I said aloud as I looked over the papers.

I was leaving her with the House, cars, and just under half a million dollars. O was being very generous considering the fact she cheated, and I have proof. After leaving the hospital, I contacted one of my tech savvy friends who hacked into Eureka's phone messages and logs. She retrieved

211

every nasty message and picture between Hen and Eureka, even captured her drug deals.

I had more than enough to get the divorce, but because of the fact of our son, I wasn't going to leave her high and dry like she deserves to be.

I continued to sign the papers and place them back inside of the envelope.

I felt a hint of sadness, I guess from the way things turned out.

This past couple of years I have suffered too many losses and setbacks and I just wanted it to be over.

The sound of my phone vibrating again agitated to me to the point that I picked it up, "WHY DO YOU KEEP CALLING! I said I did-"

"Jo'nte?"

The sound of a familiar voice caused me to settle my tone.

"Tori? Is this you?" Shocked and embarrassed, I calmed my tone. I couldn't believe my ears. Her sultry voice instantly brought me back to the days she and I would talk.

"Yes, it's me JC. How have you been?"

"It's been a long time. I'm doing okay and what about you? How have you been?" I hoped she would say the things I felt like, I missed you. I have been miserable without you, can we make what we had worked? I know it was a long shot, but I had to hold on to some hope, that this woman, this big beautiful woman would still love me the way I still loved her. So I waited for her response.

"I'm fine." She paused.

213

"I should have called you sooner, I heard about the accident. How are you and your wife?" I could hear the hint of sarcasm in her voice when she spoke the word 'wife', but she continued on.

"Tori are you okay, I hear the hesitation in your voice. I bet you are twirling the front of your hair between your fingers because you're nervous."

"JC that was so long ago. But you do know me so well." She gave a slight chuckle.

"Well, I am so sorry I haven't called before now. I want to offer my condolences concerning the death of your son. I know that was a devastating loss for you and Eureka. Again I send my love and prayers up for you. But the reason I'm calling is, I need to see you as soon as possible."

I had a feeling that something was wrong by the way she asked to see me. We haven't seen each

214

other since, right before she moved to London and that was almost two years ago.

"Hey, Tori are you sure you are okay? I heard about this Hen guy has he hurt you? What did he do to you? I swear to god if he touched you I wi-"

"JC, calm down Gangsta I'm fine. Let me find out you're about that life." She said sounding amused that I came out of my normal swag. "There are some things I need to discuss with you and I need to do it face to face. Yes, Val told me you called and told her about Eureka knowing Hennry. I had no idea that she would but never mind. I need to talk, so when will you have a moment of free time?"

"I can be out on the next flight if you need me."

"No silly, god I miss that about you. Always putting others first." Her voice drifted off as if she was in a moment in our history. This was my confirmation

215

that she still held me close in her heart and maybe just maybe she missed me all this time like I have missed her.

"I'm sorry, I'm out of line you are a married man now. My apologies. JC but please if you can come soon I would really appreciate it. The sooner the better."

"Okay, I can be there the day after tomorrow. I had a meeting set up with a new client some up and coming basketball player, his last name is Scarborough. Maybe you have heard of him? for next week, but I will give him a call to see if he can move up our meeting. That way I can kill two birds with one stone, or shall I say one long ass flight."

"O-o okay. That is fine. The day after tomorrow it is."

Hearing some disappointment and hesitation in her voice I asked her if she need me to come tonight. She told me no the day after tomorrow will be okay. But I had a feeling something was off.

While she was talking a little more and asking me about my new business, I was on my laptop booking a hotel room and a first-class flight to London for that morning. Curiosity was getting the better of me.

"Oh, Tori will I be coming to your house? Or are we meeting somewhere? I don't want your man getting mad."

"JC now you know how I am, I control me and yes we need to meet at my house."

"Okay, okay Miss Lady, what's your address?"

"336-337 the Strand London WC2R 1HA."

217

"I will never get used to their address system there. But I have it and I will see you soon."

We ended the call. I was finished booking my room and flight before she could even say the words goodbye. I was eager to see her and even more intrigued about what it was she wanted to talk to me about.

I dialed Quinten's number he answered on the first ring sounding out of breath, "A' bruh did I catch you at a bad time?"

"Nawl, nawl, I'm just getting my work out on. Whats up?"

" I need your assistance. I have to go on a business trip in the morning and I need my things moved back into my apartment. The movers were coming at 7 am and I won't be here to can you do me a solid and make sure my shit is moved up out of here. I'm not sure how Eureka is going to react when she gets served with them divorce papers and I don't want to have to put the hands on her for tearing up my stuff. I don't hit women but man she makes ah brother come real close to it."

"So you really going through with that? That's wuss up' of course I can help you out I'ma swing by in a few and pick up the keys and whatever else you need me to take care of."

"Oh come on Scoop, you were not punking out me? Let's finish this last set." I heard a female's voice in the background.

"my bag bruh... Are you working out um? Well, let me let you get back to it. I can call Joshua."

"Naw, Naw, I'm good, here I come give me a second," He said to the female.

"Naw I'm good. We just in the gym getting our fitness on is all."

"Okay, you punking out like a little girl." The female taunted him, ten I caught on to the voice.

"Is that Val? Ahhh shit, I dint know yall knew each other. What up, holding out on ya boy."

Quinten laughs, "man we been on for a lil minute. Shawty a good girl and you know I like my women BBW, type that wanna fuck you dry then eat some lunch with you." We laughed so hard after he sang the lyrics to Drake's part of the hit song 'no type'.

He agreed to come by tonight and get the keys so I can make my flight early.

I packed a small suitcase and set everything by the door.

I wasn't missing this flight, the devil himself couldn't keep me away from Tori. Not this time.

CHAPTER 23

Hell has no fury

"What do you mean he is not answering? Some body better get my husband here and now! Do you know who I am?" Eureka yelled from the top of her lungs at doctors, nurses and anyone else who came into her room.

JC had the divorce papers messengered to the hospital. The same morning Eureka was to be released. Her reaction was worse than when she removed the bandage from her face revealing the horrific scar left by the accident. After several skin grafts, the doctors had done all they were able to, to make her look almost as she did before.

"How dare him! Where is he? I WANT TO SEE HIME NOW!" In a fit of rage she tossed furniture and medical equipment around her hospital room.

"Calm down Mrs. Collinsworth, we have tried to contact your husband for you. Please think of the health of your baby." Nurse Tomas said trying to calm Eureka down.

Eureka instantly stopped, then sat down on the floor.

With tears running down her face, she looked up at Nurse Tomas with pleading eyes, "what am I gonna do now? I have lost him."

Eureka had known for a few weeks that she was pregnant. At first she was trying to kill it by taking drugs and parting hard, but then she came up with the idea to replace the child her and JC lost , by telling him she was pregnant with hi child for a

222

second time and they had another chance to be a family. But she was sure he knew about the baby because in the papers he sent for the divorce, he'd set up a trust fund for the baby when it becomes eighteen years of age he or she would receive it.

There were some many things she wanted to say to him in hopes of making everything right.

"I have to get out of here, please im sorry, I allowed my emotions to get the better of me. If you could call a cab for me to get home I would appreciate that. And again im sorry for the way I reacted."

Eureka appeared calm and polite and very apologetic, but inside the only thing she wanted was to get home, the home she shares with her still husband. In her mind if she couldn't have him no one will.

The nurse left the room and called for a cab. While waiting, her thoughts remained on JC and the life they will have.

She limped in the bathroom to look in the mirror, "all I need to do is put a little make up on and fix my hair, he will love me regardless, im still that pretty bitch he fell in love with." She coached herself. In her mind her beauty and almost perfect body would be enough to fix things with JC.

Pulling out a small container from her pocket she bent down to the faucet and took a handful of water to swallow a small white pill.

Her eyes rolled toward the ceiling as the drug took an instant affect.

224

She gave herself one more look in the mirror, there was no way she couldn't have the career the man and the wealth she desired.

Her make up bag was sitting on the stand next to the sink, she pulled out her crimson red lipstick from Macy's by the Mac collection. Combed her hair just past her face then placed a pair of wine colored Ray-ban sunglasses over her eyes.

Giving herself a onceover she smiled in delight thinking how close she came to loosing JC caused her to thank God he was going to give her another chance.

"We can renew our vows and this time I will walk down the aisle Mr. to a ton of cameras and people in a stunning dress made by Vera Wang. JC stop your smearing my lipstick. Of course you can have a kiss." She leaned and kissed the mirror, leaving a smudged print of her lips on the glass.

225

She grabbed the rest of her things and continued to pack so she could head home.

Chapter 24

Catch my heart it's yours Forever

I was so nervous. How was I going to explain to him how I decided to keep our daughter, his only child from him? I tossed and turned all night thinking of the right words to say to JC.

I hope I get the chance to tell him before Eureka tells him. Being deceptive has never been the way I live my life, because I know all too well the hurt lies and deceit can cause to your heart.

'One more day until I tell him. Lord give me the strength.' I prayed inwardly as I noticed the time was getting closer for me to wake Samya up and we get our day started. Hennry has left me over a thousand messages, all pleading and begging. I told him what Eureka said to me about how and why he hooked up with me.

He tried to deny it and even hit me with some lame excuse but I wasn't falling for it. The fact that I was just starting to relax and give in to the idea that I could really be close to another man other than JC really hurt when I found out the truth. But I was thankful I hadn't introduced him to my daughter.

Not really able to drift back off to sleep, I rolled out of the bed to go into Sue-Sue's room. I stood in her doorway and watch her sleep peacefully. I thank God for blessing me with this little person who has a big impact.

227

I could hear my cellphone ringing from the other room, "hello." I said before the sound could wake up my baby.

"Look fat bitch... tell my husband he has one hour to get home before I make you and bastard pay."

"Eureka is this you? Are you high? Your husband lives with you why would he be all the way here. Girl get you a grip on reality you starting to look pathetic. And why would he be here again, what you told him about my baby?"

"Tori, you busted can of biscuit lookin bitch, stop playing. Now put him on the phone. When I got out of the hospital and arrived at my house, all of his stuff was gone. All he left was something with your name and a bunch of scribble on some paper. Tori he is my husband, do you want to add home wrecking whore onto your resume. Isn't enough that you have his bastard child, now you want him to? You big bi...."

"See I have warned your slow ass. I hope he does come so I can show him what he's been missing. All these thighs you refer to as fat, baby , honey he had the time of his life inside of them , oh and so did Hennry seems he can't get enough of this fat bitch either. May be I should write a book for you so called smart pretty bitches, I think I will and title it 'How to keep my man a BBW love story." I started laughing hard after hearing screaming through the phone.

"Tell all that to this."

"To what?"

"The click." And I hung up in her face. I was so mad, but even more upset with myself because I allowed her to once again take me there.

229

Walking over to the cupboard in the kitchen, I grabbed a coffee mug and poured me a nice cup. Forgetting that I hadn't brushed my teeth I rushed back upstairs to my bathroom.

"That damn Heffa. Don't know when to leave things alone. I can't stand weak females." I said angrily brushing my teeth. I gripped the tooth brush so hard out of anger that I almost broke it. I wanted so badly for that to be my hands around Eureka's neck. I heard my doorbell ring, so I hurried to finish before it woke up Samya.

"Who is it?" I chimed out. There no answer s so I stepped to the door and looked out of the peep hole. I could see the top of a hat. Thinking it was my neighbor I open the door, "Mr. Gra..." I stopped cold when I was looking into the face of JC.

"Hey lady, are you gonna invite me in?" he smiled from ear to ear. Looking every bit of my daughter. I could see her round face and button sized nose all in his face. And that is the same smile she gives me every day. This was making it harder now that he is herein person.

"Ye-yes come in."

"Thank you, I see the weather hasn't changed here much. Still foggy and cold. So how have you been?" he leaned in to kiss my cheek. The touch of his soft lips against my skin caused me to reminisce briefly about us, the way we use to be.

"Would you like some coffee? I was just about to drink a cup myself.

X…………X

231

I stood in her doorway looking at the love of my life. No matter how much time had passed she was just as beautiful as the day I met her. When she let me inside, it took all I had not to kiss her lips so I chose the closet part of her to her lips. The scent of her lavender body wash was still one of my favorites. It was something about the way it mixed with her natural scent, made it exotic to me.

"Sure I will have a cup. I love your home. You decorated it yourself?" I placed my coat on the side of her couch and looked around a little. Not wanting seem pushy I looked at the art work she had on the walls. Then on the mantel I spotted a picture of a baby.

Not wanting to pry, I asked, "So what was so important that I needed to get to you ASAP. I was going to wait until tomorrow but you know me better than that. I heard it in your voice you needed me so im here. So whats up?"

She looked at me with some sadness and fear.

"Please come have a seat. I have to tell you something.

X........X

I couldn't find the words. As he sat down, all I could do to keep from kissing him was focus on the task at hand. How am I going to tell him about Samya? Will he be mad? Will he hate me?' so many thoughts ransacked my mind. My hands nervously shook as I poured his cup of coffee.

233

"Baby you okay? Why are you shaking?" he reached over and placed his hand over mine to calm me, but tears started to run down my face. He looked even more concerned as he rubbed my hand. Seeing the tears came down more, he got up and came to my side of the table and hugged me.

"Tori, whatever it is we can face it together. Please let me help you."

"Jon'te Im, im so...rrryy. Please forgive me. I didn't know how to tell yo..."

Just as I was about to get it out Samya started crying. I jumped back from him and ran to my baby's room.

X.........X

234

I rushed behind her. I made it up to what looked like a child's room. "Tori is everything alri-" I was looking into the face of one of the prettiest little girls I'd ever seen. Her hair was curly and eyes were a dead giveaway. I slowly walked over to Tori and the child she was holding trying to console.

"Shh, shh, its okay mommy's here." Tori cradled the baby in her arms.

"Tori, did you say mommy? Is this your baby?"

"No she is ours. Jon'te meet your daughter Samya."

"How? When? Why you didn't tell me? Tori why?"

I shot question after question out of confusion and shock.

"Let me take her down to breakfast and I will explain then."

235

I held my hand out, "can I hold her?"

Tori looked up at me with tears ain her eyes, "yes."
She said as she slowly handed me my daughter.

When I took one look at this baby I knew she was
mine. But now holding her up close it was really
confirmed, I didn't need a DNA test to tell me what
I already knew. She had the same birth mark on her
left shoulder as mine.

"Hey lil momma, hi, hi im your daddy. What did
you say her name was again?' I asked angry at the
fact that my daughter didn't know me and I didn't
know her.

"Samya is her name."

"Tori does she at least have my last name?'

"No JC I felt it would be bes-"

"Never mind, Samya hi little lady im daddy." I kissed her forehead with tears falling s down my face. She looked at me confused then tried wiping my tears. Her innocence was touching and the way she cared for me, a total stranger to her reminded me of my mother.

I hugged her a little closer to my chest. For the second time in my life I cried like a girl. Once when my son died and now holding my daughter.

"Im sorry JC im sorry!"

Tori rushed out of the room crying startling the baby. I could tell it was hurting her, watching me with our daughter. I stayed in my daughter's room for hours watching her and playing with her. Hearing her baby chatter had me angry allover. Just thinking about all of the lost moments I will never get back with her.

237

Her first words, her first steps and even the first time she held a spoon to feed herself.

With my emotions all over the place I didn't know what to do, should I go and curse Tori out or thank her for blessing me with this beautiful little girl that we made out of love.

CHAPTER 25

Make it like it was… no better than before

Tori sat on the patio staring off into an abyss. Seeing JC and Samya together for the first time really had her messed up in the head. Her heart was crushed and happy at the same time as if that was possible.

Haring footsteps coming down the stairs She knew things were about to get even deeper. The time had come that she had to tell JC everything.

When he got to the doorway he was still holding Samya. Playing and cooing with her. They both were smiling. She even giggled as he tickled her sides.

Tori's mocha complexion was rosebud red from shame and guilt.

JC sat down in the chair next to Tori with Samya on his lap,

"Are you ready to talk?" he said sternly.

Not wanting to look at the hurt in his eyes Tori spoke facing the opposite direction, "yes, I will call for the sitter to watch her while we talk.

"Sitter? No, she can stay right here with me. I have already missed out on so much time with her I don't want to let her out of my sight. We can talk as a family together."

The forcefulness in his tone warned Tori this was not up for a debate. Feeling defeated and full of

240

guilt she agreed and began telling him when she found out about her pregnancy and when and why she decided to move to London.

"So why didn't you just come to me. Tori I would have done anything for you, for her for us. Tori I love you. I loved you then and I still love you now."

"Jon'te there were so many days I wanted to pick up the phone and call you. To let you know, we were having a child. And that no matter what I loved you. I even picked up the phone a few times, dialed your number anonymously just to listen to your voicemail, to hear your voice so I would never forget. Every day I thought about the what if's and why nots of our whole situation, but the same thing would always happen, I would come right back to the same reality, you'd just lost your son and you were married to her." The sadness in Tori's voice causes JC to loosen up his tone.

241

Samya reached for her mother to hold her. Tori turned and placed her in her arms out for her.

JC was so impressed by the love Tori shows their daughter. She held on to her a si f she was a glass and could break at the slightest touch.

JC stood up and walked dot the edge of the patio deck, "Tori were you ever going to tell me? Or was it because Eureka found out is why I know now about my daughter, my baby, Tori our baby. We made her out of love. I know I didn't handle the situation with Eureka the way I should have and I owed you better. I thought you moved away for the same reasons I wanted you to stay. I couldn't take seeing you and couldn't touch you. I knew it wasn't fair to you and you deserved so much better. Eureka really brought a lot of dramas and crazy onto my life and yours. But Tori I still had a right to be a part of our child's life."

242

For the first time he was truly upset with Tori. He'd never shown her anything other than kindness and empathy, because that is what she'd shown him. But this was a low blow to him, especially coming from her. If anyone he thought would always be up front with him, it would be her.

"JC to be completely honest with you, I don't know if I would have told you."

"What the hell do you mean? She is my da-"

"Hear me out. At that time, everything was all new to me. When I found out that I was pregnant all I could think of was how I am going to raise a child with someone who belongs to someone else Before the baby and all of that, I thought you and I were making a start at something wonderful; when she dropped the bomb on you, then on top of that your son died, then you married her, I was not

243

about to let that bitch anywhere near my child. I'm sorry, but she is a piece of work.

JC, I loved, no love you and seeing you today made me realize I was wrong for keeping her away from you. Can you please look at it from my side and forgive me? Please"

When Tori's tears fell down her cheeks JC was so wrapped up in the remorse that adorned her face he softened his thinking and decided to stand up in front of her along with Samya, "yes Tori I forgive you. Although I'm mad, but I do understand." He both she and Samya a hug.

They talked some more and decided to start over, with no lies or secrets.

Epilogue

Months passed.....

After JC and Tori talked things out they decided it would be best to raise their daughter in the United States.

After months and months of planning, it was almost time for Samya's 3rd birthday and they both wanted this to be a party she would always remember.

Tori went all out, she hired one of the Disney princess's characters to be a part of the party, a Dj and even had one of the chefs from the hit show

'Cake Boss' design and make an elaborate cake for the party.

She spared no expense when it came to Decorations and food and JC matched her.

They rented the entire amusement park for that day and invited tons of celebrity children.

When Tori thought of how things were so much better now that JC was in Samya's life.

"Da-da, mine. Pw-ease…." Hearing Samya call, JC dad brought smiles to his face. She had him wrapped around her little fingers. If he was a lollipop she has him in her pocket. He was very over protective over her.

Eureka would drive past their office building and made threats to hurt Tori and Samya, JC hired a private security firm to give them added protection.

JC and Tori decided to take things slow when it came to them and their relationship. Although she still used Hennry's Real girls have curves collection 'and brought it back to the states. They were a hot seller for plus sized women who desired to be sexy and feel confident in their appearance. The models were fully figured and fabulous.

Hennry stayed in London. He tried calling Tori many times but each time she sent him right to Voicemail. It had gotten so bad that Tori changed her number.

Getting everything prepared Val noticed a black car off to the right side of the street. At first she didn't pay a lot of attention to it that was until it was still there four hours later.

247

She went to tell JC and his security team.

As they rushed over toward the car it sped off. All JC could see was two figures in the front seats.

Tori came running outside with Samya in her arms.

"JC did you see who that was?"

"No, but let's get you both back inside. I have a feeling that was Eureka and she wasn't alone."

Hearing JC sound a little rattled, Tori took the baby back inside. For the rest of the party, everything was safe. The kids enjoyed themselves.

JC felt better having Tori and Samya stay at his house for the night.

"Thank you, JC for letting us stay the night."

"No need to thank me, we are family. And you know our daughter is my world."

Not able to look JC in the eyes, Tori looked away for a moment.

"It's okay baby girl we have worked through a lot of this together and I forgive you. Come on you would think after the few times we have made love you would have gotten past this." He lightly chuckled.

"I am, but we are right back at that same moment when Eureka changed our lives forever, but this time I am going to let you know. JC I went to the doctor the other day, remember that one night after we took Sue-sue out to Chucky cheese? And you and I ended up making love?' He inched a little closer towards me.

"How could I forget? I never felt so close to you. Tori you are still in my heart."

249

"Well I'm in your heart and in your life forever, JC we are about to give Sue-sue a little brother or sister. I'm pregnant." He took a small step back.

"For real? Are you serious? Tori please don't play. Ma I really love you and this would be the third best thing that has happened to me in my whole life. The first was meeting you and, of course, our daughter now this, my son. My life is so complete.

"Son? How are you so sure? I'm only a few weeks along."

"I just know. Oh my God. Tori I'm so ha..."

Hearing a clapping sound, Tori and JC turned to see a dissolved Eureka standing in JC's living room clapping her hands with Hennry right on her side. JC was quickly put Tori behind him to shield her from the gum Eureka held in her hand. Hennry with glossy eyes stood in silence holding a gun of his own.

"So you all are one big happy family? I see fat bitches winning. JC you left me high and dry for her and that started lookin ass little girl."

JC was about to lunged at her, but Tori came from behind him and punched Eureka in the mouth.

"I told you, you didn't have one more time to disrespect my child." Eureka hit the floor when she turned over the gun went off.

Tori fell to her knees and blood spewed from her arm.

"GET THE FUCK DOWN!" Hennry yelled.

"This simple bitch shot me," Tori screamed in agony as Hennry hit JC in the head with the butt of his gun.

251

He snatched Tori up by her hair and dragged her to the edge of the balcony. JC struggled to regain his balance. Eureka stood to her feet then rushed toward Hennry and Tori. JC dashed in their direction too.

Grabbing Hennry by the throat JC tossed him to the ground off of Tori. He was so busy hitting henry with his fist in a mad rage.

"You sick bastard," JC yelled.

When he turned his head to the side he noticed Eureka and Tori fighting. Tori kicked Eureka in the face then Eureka hit Tori causing her to hang on the top of the balcony rail.

Tori struggled to hang on, but Eureka was pushing her by the feet. Tori held on to Eureka, trying to pry her hands off of her.

"Mommy, da-da." Both Tori and JC heard Samya calling for them as she stood in the middle of the living room. Turning her head, Tori lost her balance, "NOOO! NOOO!" JC yelled. As Tori's body fell over the railing.

She held on tight to Eureka's shirt and pulled her over with her. Both of them hit the top of a parked car. JC ran to edge in shock trying to grasp at Tori, but he was too late.

With tears running down his face, he rushed and picked Samya up and hurried down the elevator. By the time he made it to Tori, her body was broken but a smile adorned her face.

CPSIA information can be obtained at www.ICGtesting.com
Printed in the USA
LVOW07s1632130116

470477LV00018B/1016/P

9 781517 575816